From #1 *New York Times* bestselling phenomenon Sylvia Day comes a hotly anticipated and passionate new love story.

Once, I would never have imagined myself here. But I'm settled now. In a place I love, in a home I renovated, spending time with new friends I adore, and working a job that fulfills me. I am reconciling the past and laying the groundwork for the future.

Then Garrett Frost moves in next door.

He's obstinate and too bold, a raging force of nature that disrupts the careful order of my life. I recognize the ghosts that haunt him, the torment driving him. Garrett would be risky in any form, but wounded, he's far more dangerous. I fear I'm too fragile for the storm raging inside him, too delicate to withstand the pain that buffets him. But he's too determined . . . and too tempting.

And sometimes hope soars above even the iciest desolation.

Emotional and heartrending, *Butterfly in Frost* marks a brilliant return by global sensation Sylvia Day, the #1 international multimillion bestselling author of the Crossfire saga.

PRAISE FOR SYLVIA DAY

"You know you're in for a good book when other authors—and I mean LOTS of other authors—recommend it."

—USA Today

"A page-turner!"

—Access Hollywood Live

"Glamorous people, swanky settings, steamy sex, and passionate married love make this a heartwarming, gratifying conclusion to the series."

—Publishers Weekly

"[A] highly charged story that flows and hits the mark."

—Kirkus Reviews

"Will have you furiously flipping pages."

—Glamour

"Sophisticated, engaging, clever and sweet."

—The Irish Independent

"Superb writing . . . I can't wait to see what Day does next!"

—RT Book Reviews

"When it comes to brewing up scorchingly hot sexual chemistry, Day has few literary rivals."

—*Booklist*

"Day writes indulgent fantasy at its most enjoyable, in a story populated by high-society beauties and rakes, all of them hiding dark passions and darker secrets behind their glittering facades."

—*Shelf Awareness*

"This bold, erotic tale of passion and revenge features a cast of colorful characters and a complex and intriguing plot."

—*Library Journal*

butterfly
in
frost

OTHER BOOKS BY SYLVIA DAY

Contemporary Romance

The Crossfire® Saga

Bared to You
Reflected in You
Entwined with You
Captivated by You
One with You

The Jax & Gia Series

Afterburn/ Aftershock

Paranormal Romance

The Renegade Angels Series

A Dark Kiss of Rapture
A Touch of Crimson
A Caress of Wings
A Hunger So Wild

The Dream Guardians Series

Pleasures of the Night
Heat of the Night

Historical Romance

The Georgian Series

Ask for It
Passion for the Game
A Passion for Him
Don't Tempt Me

Urban Fantasy

The Marked Series

Eve of Darkness
Eve of Destruction
Eve of Chaos
Eve of Warfare
Eve of Sin City

Single Titles

The Stranger I Married
Seven Years to Sin
Pride and Pleasure
In the Flesh

Omnibus

Spellbound
Scandalous Liaisons
Love Affairs

Novellas

The Shadow Stalkers Miniseries

Razor's Edge
Taking the Heat
Blood & Roses
On Fire

The Carnal Thirst Series

Misled
Kiss of the Night

All Revved Up
"Mischief and the Marquess" in *Perfect Kisses*
"Hard to Breathe" in *Premiere*

butterfly
in
frost

a novella

SYLVIA
DAY

Text copyright © 2019 by Sylvia Day, LLC
All rights reserved.

Published by Montlake Romance, Seattle

www.apub.com

Amazon, the Amazon logo, and Montlake Romance are trademarks of Amazon.com, Inc., or its affiliates.

ISBN-13: 9781542016735
ISBN-10: 1542016738

Author photo © 2019 by Meghan Poort

Cover design by Caroline Teagle Johnson

Printed in the United States of America

To the Tabke family,
for inspiring me with your strength,
compassion, and faith

1

"It's barely nine a.m., and I'm already tipsy."

My neighbor Roxanne, who's just thrown her front door wide open in response to my knock, stands before me with a gleam in her eye. Her two dogs, a loudly barking Weimaraner and an even louder Corgi-Chihuahua mix, rush out to greet me.

"What's the occasion?" I drop into a crouch and brace myself for the onslaught of warm, furry bodies. Looking up, I note the jeans hugging Roxy's mile-long legs and the classic white button-down shirt she's knotted at the waist. As always, she makes flawless look effortless.

She grins down at me. "Mondays are for mimosas, Doctor."

"Is that right?" I give both dogs a thorough rubdown, flattered by their delight at my arrival. "Don't expect an argument from me. I've been known to prescribe a drink or few now and then."

"But *you* never drink."

I shrug. "Because I'm not a fun drunk. I just get maudlin."

The fervent welcome Bella and Minnie are giving me prompts her to say, "They missed you. I missed you, too."

"I wasn't gone long enough to be missed." As I stand, I congratulate myself for somehow managing to avoid the twin madly licking tongues.

My breath rushes out when Roxy grabs me in a fierce hug. She's five inches taller, several years older, and miles ahead of me in glamour and beauty.

Pulling back, she studies me, then comes to some sort of conclusion with a nod. My gaze slides over the riot of shoulder-length curls framing her oval face. She's got brown eyes several shades lighter than her skin, and they shine with the kindness of a genuinely sweet soul.

"How's Manhattan?" she asks as she links arms with me and pulls me into the house.

"As frenetic as ever."

"And my favorite celebrity couple?" She kicks the door shut behind us. "Are they still gorgeous and glamorous and filthy rich? Is she pregnant yet? You can tell me; I won't tell a soul."

I smile. I missed Roxy, too. She's a gossip but never malicious about it. Still, she can't keep a secret beyond five minutes.

"Yes, Gideon and Eva Cross are still amazing in every way. And I'm not Eva's doctor, so I can't say if she's expecting or not. In any case, as good as you are at ferreting out info, I expect you'd know as soon as she did."

"Ha! If only. Kylie Jenner's hidden pregnancy proved even famous people can have secrets." Her eyes brighten with excitement. "So maybe Eva's expecting and keeping it under wraps."

I hate to disappoint her, but . . . "For what it's worth, there was no visual evidence of a baby bump."

"Damn it." Roxy pouts. "Oh well. They're young."

"And busy." As someone who works for them, I know that firsthand.

"What was she wearing when you saw her? I want a full recap: outfit, shoes, accessories."

"Which outfit?" I ask innocently. "I saw her more than once."

Her eyes light up. "Ooh, girl. Let's have lunch at Salty's so you can tell me everything!"

"I could be persuaded," I tease.

"In the meantime . . ." Her lush perfume fades as she moves into the living room. "I've got a lot to catch you up on."

"I've only been gone three weeks. How much could possibly happen?"

I follow Bella and Minnie to the edge of the living room, instantly feeling settled in the familiar place. Decorated mostly

3

in white with pops of navy and gold, the traditional style of Roxy's home is both elegant and comfortable. Scattered here and there are vividly colored mosaic pieces—coasters, decorative bowls, vases, and more—which she creates and has employees sell at Pike Place Market.

But it's the expansive view of Puget Sound beyond her windows that steals the show.

The panorama of the Sound, along with Maury and Vashon Islands, stops me in my tracks. A giant red-and-white barge weighted with stacks of multicolored shipping containers rumbles carefully away from Tacoma, slowing in preparation for the sharp pivot required to exit from Poverty Bay. A tugboat, looking so tiny in comparison, chugs in the opposite direction. Private boats, ranging in size from dinghies to cabin cruisers, dot the anchorages near the shore.

Gazing at the glittering water and the vessels that come and go at all hours is something I never tire of. In fact, I missed this view terribly while in New York.

And to think, I'd once sworn that just as I had been born in the Big Apple, I would also die there. I'm definitely not the woman I used to be.

I check the giant old-growth tree on the edge of the bluff for the telltale bright white of a bald eagle's head. The bare branch that serves as a favorite perch is empty now, but in the distance, a row of planes descending into SeaTac Airport from the north tells me which way the wind is blowing. I turn back to watch Roxy finish sliding her feet into spotless white walking shoes.

She stands. "So you know you missed the get-together—again. I don't think you've been to one since the holidays, have you?"

I slide around the corner to escape the question and grab the dogs' leashes hanging on wall hooks in the front hallway. "I mean, did I really *miss* anything? I'm thinking no."

Every month, A-frame signs appear on our streets, announcing the date and location of the next community gathering, a useful reminder when planning my work trips to New York. Gatherings of people are problematic for me and best avoided when possible.

"Emily showed up with her gardener." Roxy joins me, clipping a carabiner holding a tube of biodegradable poop-scoop bags to her belt loop. "They're dating now, if that's what you call it."

The news makes me pause, peripherally aware of the dogs now spinning around with excitement. "The kid? Isn't he, like, sixteen?"

"God." Roxy's laugh is a throaty delight. "He almost looks it, doesn't he? He's actually twenty."

"Yikes." Emily is a bestselling novelist who recently went through a painful divorce. Having experienced that myself,

I wish her the best. It's unfortunate that a recent string of boyfriends the same age as her son is scandalizing our neighborhood.

"Trauma can really screw people up." As sympathetic as I am, I'm careful not to reveal too much of that sentiment in my voice.

We all wear armor in different ways. Mine is reinvention.

"Listen, I get it. But bringing your boy toy—especially one who mows some of your neighbors' lawns—to the community potluck is just dumb. The looks she was getting when her back was turned . . . hoo-wee."

We both bend to attach the leashes.

"The things I miss," I jest, making a mental note to send Emily a *thinking of you* card.

"That's not all."

"Oh?" I take Minnie while Roxy takes Bella. We've never specifically agreed on that arrangement; it's just our routine. Just as walking the dogs together a couple of times a week is routine—a scheduled interaction that gets me out of the house and into the sunshine, per my doctor's orders.

Roxy bounces on her feet with excitement. "Les and Marge sold their house."

I blink. "I didn't know they were selling."

She laughs and heads toward the front door. "That's the thing. They weren't."

"Wait, what?" I hurry after her as she steps outside, Minnie running alongside me, keeping her tail clear of the door as I shut it.

I look to the right at my home, a lovingly restored butterfly-roofed midcentury, then on to the traditional house just beyond it that belongs—*belonged*—to Les and Marge. Including Roxy's, all three of our homes have unique lots set between the homes that line the street and the Sound, affording us unhindered views of the water as well as exceptional privacy—all within a twenty-minute drive of the airport.

Roxy shortens the length of her stride to allow me to catch up, then glances over at me. "The day after you flew to New York, a Range Rover pulled into their driveway, and the guy inside offered them cash to close—and move out—in fourteen days."

My step falters, and Minnie gets momentarily tangled in her leash. The dog shoots me what I would describe as an irritated look, then keeps trotting forward. "That's crazy."

"Isn't it? Les wouldn't say how much the offer was, but I'm thinking it was huge."

We march up the inclined driveway, my head tilted back to take in the houses scaling the hillside. Designed with big windows to maximize the view, the homes have a look of wide-eyed wonder. Our little stretch of the Sound used to be a secret, but with the housing boom taking over Seattle and Tacoma, we've been discovered. Many residences are undergoing major renovations to suit the tastes of new owners.

Reaching the road, we turn left. To the right is a dead end.

"Well, if they're happy," I say, "I'm happy for them."

"They're overwhelmed. It was a lot to happen all at once, but I think they're happy with their decision." Roxanne stops when Bella does, and we wait as the two dogs mark one of their usual spots on the gravel edging the asphalt. There are no curbs on the streets in our neighborhood and no sidewalks. Just beautiful lawns and a profusion of flowering shrubs.

"We all tried prying information out of them," she goes on, "but they weren't sharing anything about the sale." She gives me a sidelong glance. "But they did share a bit about the buyer."

"Why are you looking at me like that?"

"Because Mike and I both think the buyer is someone famous. A film director maybe. Or an artist. Can you imagine? First Emily, a bestselling author. Then you, a reality-TV surgeon. Now this guy! Maybe we're sitting on the new Malibu—beachside living without wildfires or state income tax!"

The mention of Roxy's husband, Mike, coaxes an inner smile. A New York transplant like me, he adds a welcome touch of the life I left behind to the reality I've since created for myself—a reality that's just been rocked by the loss of neighbors I like.

"What are the clues you're working with?" I ask, deciding to play along. If I've learned anything over the past year, it's to accept the things I cannot change. A tough task for a control freak like me.

"Les pointed out to this guy that he hadn't even seen the inside of the house. The guy said he didn't need to. He knew already that 'the light is perfect.' I mean, who would say that? Gotta be someone who's in visual arts, right?"

"Maybe," I agree tentatively, disquieted by the unexpected conversation. The road rises sharply before us, the incline steep enough to put a little burn in my thighs. "Doesn't mean he's famous, though."

"That's the thing." Her words carry a note of breathlessness. "Les wouldn't give numbers, but he did say it was crazy the guy didn't just buy that huge compound at the end of the street. That house is listed for three and a half million!"

My mind staggers at the thought. Les and Marge have—*had*—a beautiful home, but it's not worth anywhere near that much.

"I think I saw the buyer once through that big arched window in the living room," Roxy goes on. "The blonde with him was a looker. Supermodel skinny with legs for days."

I'm panting when we reach the top; Roxy, who hits a gym most days of the week, is not.

A quarter mile farther, there's a street to the right leading to Dash Point. Beyond that and straight ahead, the road slopes back down and around until it's at water level. Redondo Beach is there, as is Salty's, a restaurant on stilts in the water with expansive views of Poverty Bay and beyond. I'm about to wax poetic about Salty's seafood chowder when a runner dashes around the corner at a full sprint. His sudden appearance rattles me. A closer look makes me freeze midstride. My breath locks in my lungs.

There are too many things to register at once, so my mind attempts to absorb the whole man. Dressed only in black shorts and shoes, he is a visual feast of deeply tanned skin, intricate sleeves of tattooed art, and sweat-slicked, flexing musculature.

And his *face*. Sculpted. Square-jawed. Brutally, breathlessly handsome.

Roxy, now a few feet in front of me, gives a low whistle. "Hot damn."

The sound of her voice reminds me to breathe. My skin feels hot and damp with perspiration. My pulse has quickened beyond what I could blame on exertion.

He doesn't see us at first, even though he's running in our direction. His mind is elsewhere, his body on autopilot. His long, strong legs devour the asphalt beneath his feet. His arms swing in a rhythmic, controlled tempo. It's impressive how gracefully his body moves at such speed, aerodynamic and efficient. There's both beauty and power in the effortlessness of his stride, and I. Can't. Stop. Staring. I know I'm doing it and should look away, but I *can't*.

"Are you seeing this?" Roxy asks, apparently unable to look away, either.

Our trances are broken by frantic barking. Bella and Minnie have spotted the stranger running full tilt in our direction.

"Hey," Roxy corrects Bella, pulling her closer. "Knock it off."

But *I'm* still too absorbed to react in time. Minnie decides to run for it. Her leash slides out of my hand as if I didn't have a grip on it at all. She's gone before I can catch her, her stubby legs moving so fast that they're a blur, on a collision course with *him*.

"Damn it." Now I'm running toward him, too, and he sees me. He shows no surprise when he's pulled from his thoughts to find two gawking women and their out-of-control dogs. The hard line of his mouth tightens as he shifts from looking distracted to laser focused. And he doesn't slow down.

Primitive instinct spurs me to evade, escape. He's like a raging cyclone hurtling toward me, and self-preservation demands retreat.

"Minnie!" I shout, swiping a hand down toward the leash while running. I miss the target. "Damn it."

"Minnie Bear!" Roxy snaps, and the tiny dog instantly skids to a halt and pivots to run back to her human.

I'm nearly as agile. I shift direction to dodge the man who's charging at me, crossing to the other side of the street.

"Teagan!"

Roxy's panicked shout of my name turns my head . . . just in time to see the Chrysler 300 barreling straight for me.

Adrenaline spurts, and I surge forward, the sound of squealing brakes raising the hairs on the back of my neck. I'm hit from behind with enough force to propel me off the road and onto my neighbor's lawn.

Winded and still terrified, it takes a few seconds to realize I'm okay.

And that the hot, hard, sweaty hunk of a man I'd been running from is on top of me.

2

"Are you fucking crazy?" he snaps, glaring down at me.

I recognize that he's beyond angry. Also that he's even more gorgeous up close.

His eyes are beautiful hazel, emerald green with bursts of gold radiating from the center. He's got ridiculously thick eyelashes, so full and dark that it's almost as if he's wearing eyeliner. His brows, too, are strong and bold, arching over those luminous, furious eyes. He's got cheekbones I'd kill for and lips that are pursed into a tight, stern line.

He shakes me. "Are you listening to me?"

I am, yes, analyzing the husky gruffness in his voice. *Jazz bar,* I think. His speech is flavored with whiskey and tobacco.

He's straddling me, dripping sweat on me, and I feel like I'm attached to a defibrillator, with sharp painful currents jolting my entire body to life. My chest is heaving with the harshness of my breathing, and every breath carries his scent. Citrus and pheromones and hardworking, healthy male.

"Teagan," he growls, pulling me up by my shoulders. "Say something."

Biceps—holy shit is the man *built*—and pectorals flexing under inked skin and rows of abs.

"Teagan." Roxy stands at his shoulder, fighting to hold Minnie and Bella back. The girls may be a different species, but they want to crawl all over him, too. "What the hell were you thinking?"

He lowers me back to the ground and stands. "She wasn't."

Looking up at him reminds me of how tall he is. He thrusts a hand at me, and I reach for it without thinking, feeling it a moment later when his skin touches mine and a spark of awareness hits me harder than his tackle. He hauls me up, then yanks his hand away, rubbing it absently across his chest.

"I've got better things to do than watch you get splattered all over the road," he tells me, his tone glacial.

There's nothing soft about this man. Not his body or personality. Not his face, which is far too masculine to be beautiful but somehow is anyway. And certainly not his incredible magnetism. That surprises me most of all, the sexual tension arcing between us.

I rub my palm, too, still feeling a residual tingling. "Well then, thanks for the save."

"Yes, thank you," Roxy says, her hand over her heart. "Scared me half to death."

His gaze bores into me. "Are you okay?"

"I'm fine." Except my hair's in a messy braid, my face is bare, and my eyebrows need taming. All of which makes me self-conscious. I wish I looked more pulled together. Appearance can be armor, too.

That's what his tattoos bring to mind, I grasp—warrior's armor. His ink drapes over his broad shoulders to cover his pectorals and shoulder blades before running down those impressive arms.

Shoving one hand through his hair, he turns his back to me and walks away.

"Hey, I'm Roxanne, by the way." And she's using the tone of voice that lets him know he's treading a fine line.

He pivots back around with his hand extended, once again displaying that powerful grace. His temper runs hot, but everything else about him is as cool as ice. "Garrett."

"Nice to meet you, Garrett." She shakes his hand, then sweeps her arm toward me. "And this reckless lady is Dr. Teagan Ransom."

Garrett's eyes narrow on her; then he shoots a disbelieving look at me. When he turns his attention back to Roxy, it's a decisive dismissal. "Keep your friend out of the street, Roxanne."

Then he's off and running, disappearing over the edge of the road as quickly as he'd appeared.

Roxy and I both stare after him. Bella and Minnie run to the end of their leashes, barking.

"Well," Roxy says as we step off the lawn. "That was more excitement than I was looking for this early in the day."

Shaky and disconcerted, I debate bowing out of the walk and going home.

She touches my elbow. "Are you really okay?"

"Yes." I keep walking, sticking with my routine. One step in front of the other. My heart is still beating too fast, adrenaline still high in my blood. Fight-or-flight warring with mental shock.

It's been a long time since anything reminded me that I'm a woman.

Despite the lengthy walk and a leisurely lunch, I'm still out of sorts as I stroll down the driveway to my house. I've been trying to compose myself all morning, and I'm irritated that I can't.

After all this time, I realize I haven't come as far as I believed.

As I skirt the detached garage and head up the walkway to my front door, I can't help but glance over at the sleek black

Range Rover parked at a haphazard angle in the neighboring driveway.

The hard lump of ice inside me still hurts.

I'm angry. I'd had each day planned out going forward. A new city, new friends, new routines. Half a year's worth of therapy and reconditioning, for what? My neighbors move, and I feel as if I've been deceived. As if the new life I've built came with a guarantee that nothing would change.

With conscious determination, I exhale and try to push out my anxiety with it. I pull my keys from my pocket as I approach my front door and slide one into the dead bolt. When the lock opens, I use the same key in the original mid-century doorknob that sits in the dead center of the door. Once inside, I relock them both, toss my keys on the end table, and disarm the alarm before the grace period runs out and the earsplitting siren goes off.

Going through each step in the same established order settles me some. But it's being back in my home, alone, that provides the greatest relief. I gaze longingly at the couch, so exhausted I just want to curl into the cushions and sleep forever. I know what it means to feel this tired; I know what's coming. That doesn't mean I can stop it.

Instead, I look ahead to the wall of windows overlooking the Sound. The left side of the butterfly roof wings up and over the double-sided fireplace and dining room, with clerestory windows following the graceful rise so nothing blocks the majestic view. Just beyond the verdant hump of Maury and Vashon Islands, the sprawling Olympic Mountains lie west and run south. Some days, fog conceals the range so thoroughly, it disappears. But on cloudless days like today, I can see the snowcapped peaks stretching down the coast.

I soak it in, letting the familiarity calm me. I stand in the center of my living room long enough to watch another massive cargo ship lumber by on the way to Tacoma. Sunlight glitters off the gently moving water, and crab-trap buoys bob to the rhythm.

It's quiet here, so very different from the frenetic pace and noise of New York. I could hardly hear myself think there, with life beating at me from all sides, a very busy medical practice, and an ever-present camera crew. Here, I can be alone with my thoughts, with no one to judge me or pity me or expect me to "get over it."

When my phone vibrates in my pocket, I don't even jump. My mind has escaped into a solitary space that shields me from the endless internal screaming that once threatened to drive me insane.

When I see Roxy's face on the screen, I accept the video call. "Hey."

"Hey back." She's animated, her eyes bright. "You near your tablet?"

"I can be." I walk over to where it sits on a charging cradle, grateful for the distraction.

"I'm texting you a link. Don't click through on your phone. You need a bigger screen."

The notification pops up, and I go through the motions to open the page she's sent me. I'm only mildly surprised when Garrett's eyes are the first things I see. This is Roxy, after all, and she's a bloodhound on the scent when it comes to gossip fodder.

"You move quickly," I murmur, scrolling a little so that his whole face comes into view.

Whew. The man is a heartthrob, no doubt about it. As jaded as I am, I can still be fazed by that level of tantalizingly assured masculinity.

"Well, it's not altogether hard to find someone who's been covered by the press." Her voice is filled with excitement. "And while I'll have to admit that Mike was right about him being an artist—I placed my bet on director—we were kinda both right, because Garrett Frost is both a photographer and painter. He takes these amazing black-and-white photos, then translates them into full-color abstract paintings. There's a slideshow in the article comparing the inspiration photos with the final art-work. Some of it's really mind-blowing."

The Frost Phenomenon Heats Up Art World Elite. That's the headline of a lengthy article featuring several photos of the artist himself with various celebrities I'm familiar with and others I'm not. One picture in particular captivates me, because he's smiling. As sexy as the man is regardless, he's even more so when lit by humor. Those beautiful eyes glow. Charming grooves etch his cheeks. And his lips are full and firm, a sensualist's delight.

"I can't believe you're not freaking out!" Roxy scolds. "Argh. Just because you meet famous people all the time. You're immune."

"I do *not* meet famous people all the time." And I sure as hell am not immune. Something low and deep inside me quivers when I look at his face.

"Hello? *You're* famous, *Doctor Midtown*," she counters. "And you were married to Kyler Jordan!"

I wince at the dual mention of the reality series that made me a known personality and my marriage to an actor still playing the superhero role that turned him into a global commodity. Many saw my story as a fairy tale and assumed I lived a charmed life. For a while, even I believed that.

Then the perfect picture shattered into a million sharp, painful shards.

"Anyway," Roxy goes on, "Garrett Frost looks like trouble, doesn't he? He's got bad boy written all over him."

He does. The devil-may-care vibe comes through in the confidence of his posture and the way he dresses, which is tasteful and expensive but also eclectic enough to say that fitting in isn't something he cares to worry about. "He's gorgeous and talented. I expect he doesn't hear the word *no* very often."

"Who would say it? Look at all the pictures of him with supermodels. Anyway, I may come over—"

The doorbell rings, and I curse, so lost in examining every minute detail of Garrett Frost's face and style that I am somewhere else entirely. "The doorbell just scared the hell out of me. Hang on. Someone's at the door."

I glance through the semisheer privacy blind covering the wide window overlooking my front yard and spy the UPS driver walking quickly back to his waiting truck. "I've got a package. Let me call you back."

"Okay. Talk soon."

I return my phone to my pocket and open the door, bending to pick up the box sitting on my doorstep. Excitement lifts my spirits as I note the sender: ECRA+ Cosmeceuticals—the project that kept my sanity intact over the past year.

Straightening, I hurry back inside, engaging the dead bolt quickly before heading to the kitchen for scissors. A few minutes later, I've got the contents spread out over my kitchen island, an assortment of skin care products in cream-and-gold packaging. The logo and overall design convey high-end luxury that delivers results—exactly the right look for Cross Industries' new line of skin care that bridges the gap between pharmaceuticals and cosmetics.

I carefully unseal the box of one item, trying to preserve the gorgeous packaging as much as possible. The bottle inside has me *ooh*ing with joy. Thick frosted glass shields a golden center. The sanitary airless pump is weighty gold, with a distinguishing aqua-blue band that denotes which step in the recommended skin care regimen the product falls within.

Picking up the enclosed note card, I recognize Eva Cross's handwriting.

Teagan,
We couldn't have done it without you.
Here's to a grand beginning!
Best, Eva

The smile on my face feels good. Here is proof that despite stepping away from my life's work in cosmetic surgery, I still managed to help create something worthwhile that might make someone in the world feel beautiful. And with a portion of the profits going to Eva's philanthropic Crossroads Foundation, I'm contributing in a small way to improving lives beyond just beauty.

I'm sniffing a drop of naturally scented serum on the back of my hand when I hear the unmistakable sound of a delivery vehicle's sliding door. Walking back over to the window, I see a postal service truck in my driveway. Since most USPS packages are left in the locked box up at the street, I expect it's something big and head to the door. Fact is, I do most of my shopping online, from groceries to takeout, clothes to household goods. It's just safer that way.

Grabbing my keys because the front doorknob is perpetually locked from the outside, I unlock the dead bolt and pull the door open to meet my mail carrier.

And nearly run straight into Garrett Frost.

3

"Where are you going?" Garrett demands, scowling down at me.

"Excuse me?" I feel like I crashed into him, even though I managed to avoid a collision with a quick hop back. Dressed in a fitted black T-shirt, worn loose jeans, and combat boots, he's a different guy from the one I ran into earlier. The addition of more clothes, however, does nothing to blunt his impact on me.

I ponder this, distressed to realize how affected I am. A dam only holds if it has no cracks. "We really need to stop meeting like this."

"Listen," he says, "I want a do-over."

"A what?"

"I want to forget about running into each other earlier. Let's start over."

"Start over," I repeat.

"Yes." He extends his hand to me. "I'm Garrett Frost."

I stare at his tattoo sleeve, perceiving design and texture and dimension.

Heaving an irritated breath, he grabs my hand. "And you're Dr. Teagan Ransom. Nice to meet you."

"Uh—"

"Now, invite me in."

My pulse leaps. "Why would I do that?"

"Why wouldn't you?"

Gaze narrowed suspiciously, I ask, "Did you move in next door?"

"Yep. Saw you come back a bit ago."

I wait for him to say something else, but he just stares at me intently.

"Since you didn't seem too happy about running into me," I say finally, "I'm wondering why you're here."

"No one's happy about getting blindsided." Garrett shoves his hands in his back pockets, lingering on my doorstep.

In my face.

"I had a lot on my mind," he tells me. "Work, moving here, stuff I've got to get done sooner rather than later. Seeing you running full tilt at me threw me off. Then you ended up lying beneath me a few seconds later, and I got blindsided all over again. You felt it, too."

I have to admit, I appreciate his bluntness.

He waits for me to speak, patient as a spider in a web.

"So we're physically attracted to each other," I admit cautiously, feeling like we should've taken a lot longer to acknowledge that out loud.

His mouth curves in a slow, easy smile. "We're on the same page."

"I don't think so. I think you've made a big leap from there."

"I'm about to." He crosses the threshold with that swift animal grace.

I'm off my feet, suspended, and he's tilting his head to take my mouth in a greedy openmouthed kiss that takes my breath away. My lips burn beneath the heat of his. His arm is below my buttocks like a sling; the other crosses my shoulder blades. His hand takes hold of the loose braid hanging down my back and doesn't let go. He kicks the door shut behind him.

I breathe him in, the scent of citrus and spice. His flavor slides into me with the stroke of his tongue, a low growl of lust vibrating from his chest to mine. I squirm, overcome, and realize I'm not trapped. I'm secured.

My legs circle his waist. My hands grasp the rough silk of his hair.

Tightening my thighs, I lift, forcing his head back as I rise over him. He takes my shifting weight with ease, opening his mouth wide as I deepen the kiss.

God, his lips look so firm, but they're soft. His body is as hard and hot as sun-warmed stone, but he's vibrantly alive in my arms. No matter how I move against him, he fits us together, the plains and valleys sliding into alignment, as if to prove our bodies were meant for just this.

"You smell so good," he breathes into my kiss.

In the back of my mind, a red warning light is flashing. The pounding of my heart is spurred by the sense that I'm being careless. But I find I can't let go.

Need, long dormant, is awakening inside me, latching on to Garrett with ravenous hunger. I can't get enough of his mouth, the way he tastes, the deep lashes of his tongue. He is unrestrained but so skilled. There is knowledge in the way he handles me, experience that promises pleasure too heady to resist.

He moves, and I tighten my grip, a low whimper of protest escaping before I can swallow it down. He hums assurance, pulling me closer.

The sound of my doorbell makes me jump. Garrett holds me tighter.

"Hey, it's Roxy!"

I stiffen to the point of pain, feeling two separate realities converging.

"She'll go away," Garrett murmurs, his lips at my throat.

My heart pounds. "She knows I'm here."

"So?"

"I can't just hide!"

Lifting his head, he looks at me. His mouth is a thin, furious line, his jaw set stubbornly. "Maybe you're in the shower. Maybe you're wearing headphones. Maybe you're making out with your neighbor."

Panic makes me frantic. "You don't just get to appear and disrupt everything!"

"Teagan." He sighs. "Calm the fuck down."

"Don't tell me how to feel!"

"Goddamn it." He sets me on my feet and strides toward the door.

There's a moment of relief. Then the panic flares again. I barely have time to scramble into the master bedroom before I hear the door open.

"Hello, Roxanne," he drawls. "Not a good time."

"Oh! I—how are you . . . Garrett, wasn't it?"

"I've been worse."

"How's Teagan?"

"Freaking out."

I shout down the hall at them. "I'm right here, you know!"

Pausing in front of the full-length mirror affixed to the wall by the closet, I cringe. My T-shirt and joggers couldn't be more wrinkled. My waist-length dark hair is a total disaster; my crown looks like a bird's nest. My brown eyes are dilated and blurry, and my mouth is a swollen, puffy red stain.

Garrett looks like a sex god, and I look like a junkie with really bad lip filler injections.

"You okay, girl?" Roxy calls out.

"Ah . . ." My gaze darts, looking for a miracle that can make me presentable. "Yes."

"There was a package on the porch. I'm putting it down on this ledge by the stairs."

"Okay. Thanks." I spin in an aimless, frantic circle. "And hang on. I'll be out in a minute."

"I'd like to have you over for dinner sometime," Roxy says, her tone lowered so I know she's talking to Garrett. "My husband, Mike, makes a fantastic homemade pizza."

"I'd like that, thanks."

"Tomorrow night, maybe? We're right next door."

"Sure. I'll bring the wine. Red?"

"A red would be perfect."

I growl and pull apart my braid. As soon as it gives, I comb my fingers through the gnarls on top of my head, whip the ends around, and secure them in a low knot. Then I hurry out to the living room, finding Garrett leaning nonchalantly against the open door as if my home were his.

Roxy's eyes are wide when I turn my attention to her, as is her smile. "Hey there, Miss Thang."

I roll my eyes. "Sorry."

"For what? You want to come over for dinner tomorrow, too?"

"Um . . ." I picture it, this tornado of a man spinning into the tranquility of my life. My palms grow damp. I feel like I've lost control of everything somewhere in the course of the day.

But I can't have them sharing personal anecdotes without me there. If information is forthcoming, I want to hear it.

"Sure," I say with a shrug.

"Don't look so excited about it," she chides. "Anyway, I'll be off. See you two around six? Call me later, Teagan!"

She leaves. I watch through the window as she cuts over to her yard. Leaving me alone with Garrett Frost. Again.

He strolls over, cups my face in his hands, and holds my gaze. "Where were we?"

"What? No!"

That dazzling smile reappears and blinds me; then he kisses the tip of my nose. "You're adorable, Doc. Sexy as hell, too."

"I'm going to close my eyes," I mutter, "and when I open them, this is all going to be a weird dream."

Reaching down, he circles my wrist with his fingers and lifts my hand to press my palm against his chest. My breath leaves me in a rush at the feel of his pounding heart.

"See what you do to me?" he murmurs, his gaze heavy-lidded. Just that quickly, he shifts from playful to seductive.

"You're manipulating me."

"And you're spinning circles in your head. Stay focused on what's right here, right now."

I pull away. "That would be a divorcée with clearly evidenced bad judgment. I can't keep getting swept off my feet and making the same mistakes."

Garrett's jaw takes on a familiar obstinate slant. "I'm not a mistake. And I get a clean slate. Whatever happened before, I don't have any strikes against me."

"You're making up the rules as you go," I complain.

"Teagan, we were just making each other feel pretty damn good. Can we focus on that?" He reaches for my hand, squeezes it. "You're not the only one feeling like the ground's shifting beneath their feet."

Jesus. Being with him is like being in the ring with an invisible boxer. You never see the hits coming.

He smiles triumphantly when I fail to offer another protest. He looks like a kid who's just opened the one present he really wanted, which he already knew he was getting because he'd peeked in the damn closet and ruined the surprise.

"Give me a chance to charm you, Doc."

"And fuck me."

"That too." His fingers push into the knot of hair at my nape, freeing the strands to fall to my waist. He lifts a handful to his nose, breathing in with his eyes closed. "I'm coming on strong, I know. I would say I'll slow down some, but I'd be lying, since I can't."

Right. Another of those invisible punches, knocking the air straight out of me.

"You *can't*. Is that so?" My brow arches. "Why not?"

"Don't have the patience."

"Really?" I say dryly, since it's been clear from the get-go that Garrett Frost does whatever he likes.

He holds my gaze, and I watch, riveted, as something shifts. His eyes darken with shadows. His lush mouth flattens. The skin over his cheekbones stretches taut. He is suddenly hauntingly beautiful, his dynamic sexuality disrupted by my awareness of his quiet suffering.

"Every day," he murmurs, "I push beyond my limits, just to remind myself that I'm technically still alive."

He reaches out and grasps my elbow, the light hold turning into a caress that slides down my forearm until our fingers touch. I feel the path of that contact, my bare skin tingling where his flesh brushed mine, as if the nerves are coming back to life.

My lips part on quickened breaths. Numbness has been my salvation.

"I'm tired of hurting," he says softly. "You remind me that my body can feel things other than pain."

My chest tightens. Garrett would be risky in any form, but wounded, he's far more dangerous. I fear I'm too fragile for the storm raging inside him, too delicate to withstand the pain that buffets him, even with only the most superficial of intimacies.

"Garrett . . . I . . ." I shake my head.

"I didn't mean to barge in and grab you like that. I don't regret it, but it wasn't the way I planned things to go."

"You had a plan?"

"It got blown all to hell, but the one I went with seems to be working." Bending, Garrett kisses me.

Unlike the blitzkrieg kiss he'd hit me with earlier, this one is tender. His lips are soft. Coaxing. His tongue glides along the seam of my mouth, teasing it open. He deepens the kiss with a slow, easy lick, making me shiver. A soft rumble conveys his pleasure and restrained desire.

It takes extreme effort to place my hands against the defined ridges of his abs and push him away. "Stop."

Garrett takes a step back, giving me room to breathe. He watches me, waiting.

"You want to start over," I tell him breathlessly, "try at dinner tomorrow. You know, sitting down at a meal, hanging with friends . . . the way normal people get to know each other."

"Tomorrow?" He scowls. "What about today?"

"You're going away today, because I need time to think."

He heaves a frustrated sigh, his hands going to his hips. When my brows lift, he curses under his breath and heads to the door. "You know damn well we're not normal people."

My gaze narrows. Creative minds are often too perceptive for their own good. "That may be true, but try being normal for once, Frost. Maybe you'll like it."

"I like *you*," he mutters as he turns to go. "That's the only reason I'm leaving."

~

"It's your own fault if you get caught," I whisper to myself, tip-toeing onto Garrett's porch and gingerly lowering the basket in my hands. My finger hovers over the doorbell, my pulse racing.

It's just that he's a single guy in a new house. Chances are, most of his stuff is still in boxes and he hasn't figured out where the grocery store is yet.

At least that's what I told myself when I opened the shopping app on my tablet and ordered a large bottle of San Pellegrino, Beecher's Flagship cheese, honeycrisp apples, and artisanal crackers. I arranged the items in a cloth-lined wicker basket he can reuse, along with a decent knife and a pair of tall, slim drinking glasses. I also included a list of nearby grocery stores, drugstores, gas stations, and coffee shops.

Taking a deep breath, I ring the bell. Then I run back to my house as fast as I can.

~

"You surprise me, Dr. Ransom. You really do." Roxy pauses in the act of chopping fresh basil and looks me over. Again. "One minute, you've sworn off men. The next, you've got a tousled hunk answering your door."

"Tousled hunk? You've been listening to too many romance audiobooks." For the millionth time, my gaze strays to the clock on the microwave. With each passing moment, my stomach tightens.

Her laugh lights up the room. "That's your fault. You're the one who got me into them."

"Yeah, thanks for that, Teagan," Mike yells through the open french doors. He's out on the patio, tending the wood burning in their pizza oven. "We used to listen to music. Now we listen to narrators pitching their voices to emulate the opposite sex. Why not just *read* the book?"

"I hear you. Some are better than others." I offer an apologetic smile. "You do get used to it after a while." I used to listen to music, too. Now my new normal is talk radio, podcasts, and audiobooks. Mysteries mostly. And stories with unhappy endings, which are more realistic.

I watch Mike for a minute. Standing a few inches shorter than Roxy, he's still more than a few inches taller than me. He boasts a head of thick brilliantly white hair and a distinguished face that often frames a boyish smile. Aside from making the best pizza I've ever had—he is a transplanted New Yorker, so I don't feel guilty saying that—his heart is as big as his wife's.

"So he just showed up at your door," Roxy presses.

Turning back to her, I sigh. She's rocking wide gold hoops and a red Gucci belt with white jeans and a sleeveless white blouse. As usual, she looks more elegant in denim than I've ever looked on a red carpet.

"Can we find something else to talk about?" I ask.

"Why? Garrett was looking mighty sexy when he answered the door."

There's a question in there, and I shake my head.

"No?" she queries, frowning. "Please don't tell me I screwed things up for you."

"Absolutely not. It was perfect timing. Thank you for the save." A save that was becoming more appreciated by the second.

"Teagan!" She sets down the knife.

"What? Don't look at me like that. You really expect me to have sex with a guy we just ran into a couple of hours before?"

"Why not? You're a grown woman." Drying her hands on a dish towel, she cocks a hip against the island. "If he revs your engine, take him for a spin."

"He'd have to show up first," I say tightly. "And it's pretty clear he's not coming."

Roxy finally looks at the clock on the microwave. It's quarter after seven. She looks at me, genuinely startled. "You want to call him?"

"I don't have his number, and even if I did, I wouldn't call him."

It hurts to be stood up—hurts like a bitch, actually—and I'm pissed off that I gave him the opening to hurt me. Pissed at him but mostly at myself. I know all about hot, confident, charismatic guys who can't be depended upon. That I lost my head—even for a second—with all the experience I have just means I'm an idiot.

Her lips purse. "I'll just run over there real—"

"Don't you dare." The tremor in my voice betrays me, but I keep myself together otherwise. I'd known this was coming, had been fighting against admitting it ever since Garrett failed to show up at my door to walk over with me, which wasn't something we discussed but somehow I'd expected him to. I waited until six before making the short trek alone. Nevertheless, a little part of me kept hoping until I couldn't delude myself any longer.

"Maybe he hasn't set his clocks yet. You know how it is moving into a new place."

"Don't make excuses for him, Roxy. If it was important to him, he wouldn't need a babysitter to get him here."

Mike squeezes my shoulder as he passes by. "His loss. I'm more than happy to teach him how to treat a lady. Just give me the word."

"He's not worth the effort."

"Agreed. On a side note, the oven's ready when you are, ladies."

Roxy glances at the clock again, her jaw clenching. "Fine. Let's take these out."

We load ourselves up with the bowls of toppings, while Mike pulls a baking sheet with balls of homemade dough out of the proofing drawer. We head outside, spreading everything on the outdoor kitchen counter.

A murder of crows squawks loudly, a familiar sound. There's a tree in Les and Marge's—*Garrett's*—yard where the crows gather, and when an eagle gets too close, they make sure everyone on the bluff knows how unhappy they are about it.

For the first time, I'm not on the eagle's side. I know exactly how those crows feel about the intruder.

Beyond my anger, though, is piercing disappointment. It's terrible hoping something—or *someone*—is better than it actually is. It was brutally effective torture, drawing someone out of their cage of loneliness, then slamming the door shut again.

Whether it's deliberate unkindness or just thoughtlessness, it's cruel all the same.

4

"Mike, as always, your pizza was divine."

He shoots me a look. "You didn't eat enough."

"I ate until I was stuffed," I assure him. "I'm pretty sure I'll be stuffed for days."

We walk to the front door, all three of us humans and the two dogs. Though it's almost exactly nine o'clock and still twilight hour this time of year, I'm past ready for bed. Energy, for me, is a delicate balance.

"Thank you for coming over." Mike pulls me into a tight hug. "It's always good seeing your pretty face."

"Thanks for having me." I hug Roxy, too, then give the dogs goodbye pats. "I'll see you two later."

Mike pulls the door open, and I step outside. It seems darker on the street side of the house, which faces northeast, than it does on the Sound side, which holds the lingering glow of sunset for what seems like forever. Still, I see the dark figure running across their lawn in the gloaming, and my whole body tightens.

When Garrett gets close enough for me to see the bottle of wine in his hand, I turn back to wave at Mike and Roxy, then walk right past him the moment he steps into the pool of illumination from their porch light.

"Hey, wait!" He grabs for my hand, but I shake him off. "I'm sorry. I lost track of time."

"Don't apologize to me. Roxy invited you."

"I know. Damn it."

I hear him go up the two wood steps to their porch. His voice carries as he talks to Roxy and Mike, his tone weighted with urgency. I pick up the pace, passing their detached carport, before cutting across their lawn to get to my house. My heart rate kicks into high gear when I hear footsteps behind me.

"Teagan, wait. Let me explain."

"I don't care, Frost."

He catches up and walks beside me. "Mike and Roxy invited me in; I brought good wine. Come back, have a glass, and I'll explain to all of you at the same time."

"I'm tired, I don't drink, and as I said, I don't care, so I don't need an explanation."

"You don't drink?" When I decline to answer, he goes on, "I was on a call with a friend in trouble. I thought it was earlier than it is. For God's sake, it's still light out!"

I refuse to look at him. "So it's the sun's fault you didn't set a reminder or an alarm or glance at your phone to check the time? I see."

"I fucked up." He grabs my arm when I reach the pathway to my front door, slowing me to a halt. "Okay? I screwed up, and I'm sorry."

I turn to him. His face is cast in shadow, which sets the square line of his jaw and the strong lines of his cheekbones into sharp relief.

"Yeah, you're also a liar."

Garrett crosses his arms. "I'm not lying."

"You did earlier when you said you weren't a mistake. You also don't have a clean slate." I flick my hand. "And you're still making up the rules as you go."

"So just like that," he says tightly, "you're writing me off?"

"Yep." I resume walking. "Better head back to Mike and Roxy before they write you off, too."

"I'm not giving up," he says, following me to the door. He stands at the end of the walk, watching as I unlock the door and push it open. "I can redeem myself."

"Goodbye, Garrett." I shut the door, turn the locks, then lean back against the cool wood.

His voice comes through the door, close enough to tell me he approached after I retreated. "I'm really sorry, Teagan."

Closing my eyes, I sigh. "Yeah. Me too."

~

"I was really mad at Garrett at first," Roxy tells me as she stares into the lighted vanity mirror I've set up on my Saarinen dining table. She smooths ECRA+ serum over her cheeks and forehead, turning her head from side to side. "But Mike and I forgave him. He got a call from a friend of his who's borderline suicidal—did he tell you that? Anyway, he was afraid if he hung up, she might hurt herself."

Turning my back to her, I slide my mug under the single-cup coffee brewer and wait. Can't argue with an excuse like that. I immediately feel like a royal bitch. Still, the whole situation has reminded me that I'm too vulnerable to risk more pain.

"This stuff is amazing!" she raves. "It just sank right in."

"Excellent! It wouldn't do much good if it just sat on top of your skin."

"How can I get some?"

"Pick the system you want, and I'll have it sent to you. That collection is for normal skin, but they have systems to address a variety of concerns. There should be a booklet—"

"I found it." She opens the glossy, beautifully photographed booklet and flips through it, while I pull vanilla almond-milk creamer out of the fridge. "He invited us over to his place for dinner tonight to make it up to us. You should come."

"Nope. Not happening." I return to my seat across from her.

She lifts her head up from reading, revealing glowing skin without a hint of shine. "He was dejected when he came back without you. Really crushed."

I shrug. "Why should I have to hang around longer and stay up later because he can't get somewhere on time, however noble and understandable the reason? I'm not the bad guy here, Roxanne."

"I'm not saying you are. I'm only pointing out that maybe he's not the bad guy, either."

"Regardless . . . I'm simply not interested in getting involved with anyone right now. Can we talk about something else, please?"

She shakes her head at me. "It's tough finding options as hot as your ex. How many guys can compete with a movie star? Garrett can."

"Looks aren't everything." And yet I've always seemed to fall for that first.

"Not just looks, although that certainly pertains. I'm talking about being famous and talented and wealthy. Kyler Jordan is a tough act to follow in a lot of respects. Plus, *you're* gorgeous, smart, talented, and wealthy in your own right. You're a hot-shot celebrity doctor, damn it. That probably intimidates a lot of guys, but Garrett's made of sterner stuff."

"Is he?"

"Seems to me so far."

"Hmm . . ." I sip my coffee. "Well, thank you for the pep talk. I worked hard to put myself through school and start my practice, then had the fortune—or misfortune, depending on how you look at it—of being Kyler's surgeon after his accident." Our subsequent marriage led to the creation of *Doctor Midtown*, which in turn caught the attention of Eva Cross and ECRA+. To this day, it seems incredible how my life snowballed. "But right now . . . I just wish I was healthy."

"You'll get there," Roxy says firmly.

"Not soon enough." My depressive episodes are occurring less frequently, but they're still an ongoing battle I wage daily. "I figure it's better to keep to myself than expect some poor guy to deal with my issues."

"Pfft," she scoffs. "No man is getting the short stick with you. You're a serious catch."

I huff out a laugh. "More like seriously damaged goods."

She leans over the table. "Aren't you lonely, Teagan?"

"I find myself to be scintillating company. Don't you?"

"Don't play. I really want to know."

"I've got other things on my mind most of the time."

I left everything behind when I moved to Washington, trying to get as far away from my past as I could without leaving the country. Aside from my neighbors and work colleagues, I don't have many people in my life anymore, and I'm perfectly okay with that.

"Maybe it's time to think about putting yourself out there," she suggests gently.

"I don't have the energy right now."

"A good relationship can charge you up. Give you support. Companionship. Sex, for God's sake. Don't you miss *that*?"

I didn't, I think to myself—until my body asserted its needs with desperate ferocity only yesterday. Despite how screwed up I am mentally and emotionally, I've apparently been resuscitated physically. "I can't deal with another failure, to be honest."

She's quiet for a while, but her thoughts are loud. Eventually, she says, "You never talk about Kyler."

"We divorced forever ago. There's nothing to talk about."

"You know that's unusual, right? Most women can talk an earful about their exes. All the shit they did wrong, what an asshole they were. Look at Emily. She gets in a dig about Stephen every chance she gets."

"She's still hurting."

"Honey." Roxy shoots me an arch look. "You're not? A woman doesn't take a sabbatical from men if she hasn't been hurt by one real badly."

I glance at my bare hands, the fingers free of any rings. "There's no point in looking back."

"Maybe you need to force yourself to so you can move on." Her voice softens. "I read the other day that Kyler's engaged to a producer."

"It's not a competition," I say tightly, feeling anger surge despite knowing she meant well. Everyone means well, but they have no fucking idea what they're saying. "She's managed to help him get clean, and he's a decent guy when he's sober, so I wish them well."

"I'm sorry." She lifts both hands in surrender. "I'm pushing."

And I'm on edge, which isn't her fault.

"I've just got to say this one thing," she continues. "You shouldn't be sitting on a shelf gathering dust."

The doorbell rings, and I glance at the front window. I can't see who's at the door, so I stand and move toward it. I pull the door open with a smile and get a jolt when I find Garrett standing on my doorstep.

"Hi," he greets me quietly, his expression both apologetic and wary.

Repentance doesn't make him any less self-assured. I find that very sexy, as I do the spatters of paint on his black boots.

Why does the sight of those droplets give me a little buzz?

Damn it. He's disconcerting on so many levels, not the least of which is how powerful he is physically. He couldn't look more relaxed, while radiating so much ferocious energy and intense sexuality that his magnetism crashes against me like waves on the shore.

On some primal frequency, he's signaling that he'd fuck me so hard and long that I'd forget my own name. And my body is receiving the message loud and clear.

"Garrett!" Roxy's voice is filled with genuine warmth. "How are you?"

"That depends," he replies, his gaze on me. "I'm here to grovel. I briefly debated bringing white roses as a truce offering, but I don't want you to think I'm not taking this seriously. That said, I'm happy to shower you with gifts if that helps my cause."

"All of that is completely unnecessary," I tell him briskly. "Roxy told me why you were late. I feel like an ass for brushing you off about it. Hopefully that squares us up a bit."

"Well, there's also that great gift basket you left on my porch. I didn't get a chance to thank you for that yet."

"I don't have a clue what you're talking about."

His mouth curves. "Now who's the liar?"

"Just don't get your hopes up, Frost. I've decided I'm happy being single."

His grin widens. "Okay. You can still invite me in."

"I could, yes. But I already have someone over."

"I've got to run home anyway," Roxy says. She's already on her feet and moving closer, so she's by my side before I can say anything to her. "I have an order for coasters to fill, and I gotta get to work. But I'm looking forward to dinner tonight, Garrett."

"Me too," he replies, flashing a smile at her that makes my pulse jump. He's too handsome for my own good. He looks at me. "Let's hope I can convince this one to join us."

"Good luck," Roxy says, patting him on the shoulder when she breezes by. "She's stubborn."

"Thanks for the support," I tell her, shaking my head as she winks at me before disappearing.

Garrett looks over my head into my living room. "I want to check out your house."

I sigh. Showing off my home is something I enjoy doing. It was a time capsule when I bought it, right down to the fifties-era electrical wiring, with a foundation slowly sliding toward the bluff. Preserving the home while bringing it up to modern building codes was challenging—and expensive—but the end result is something I'm very proud of. I took something broken and gave it new life.

Still, Garrett Frost is more than a curious neighbor hitting me up at the monthly community potluck. Inviting him into my home means dealing with all the undercurrents he brings with him.

His gaze drops down to me and locks on. "Invite me in, Teagan. Please."

No way anyone says no to him when he zeroes in like that. At least that's the excuse I give myself when I take a step back and wave him in with an exaggerated flourish.

5

Garrett strides in, and the whole open-concept space shrinks around him. Abruptly, my home seems smaller and more intimate. He gravitates instantly to the panoramic view that elevates my house from midcentury gem to something truly special.

I'm still standing at the door, holding it open, breathing in the lingering scent of him. I admire the shape of his silhouette against the vast sprawl of water. The way his broad shoulders taper into lean hips and long, strong legs. Even through his shirt, I can see the powerful shape of his back.

"Your view is better than mine," he says.

Staring at him the way I am, I'm inclined to say both are magnificent. But he's talking about the Sound, so . . . "We have the same view."

He shoots me a look over his shoulder. "You've got bigger windows."

I can't argue with that. Midcentury architecture is all about bringing the outdoors in, and I've got a seemingly endless expanse of glass to prove how effective that can be. "Les and Marge adored your house."

He shrugs, as if he hadn't gone to extremes to get them to sell. "It's all right."

My teeth clench. "Maybe you could've bought a house someone actually wanted to sell."

"Why settle for what's available instead of what I want?"

I take that statement in many different ways and am irritated by every direction. "Are you *trying* to be unlikable?"

"Trying? No." Garrett turns in a slow, easy circle. His gaze roams over everything, settling on the artwork hanging on the wall above my couch.

"She's a local artist," I tell him.

"Hmm." He turns away. "I didn't evict your neighbors. They named their price; I paid it."

"You don't know how much they loved that place."

"They loved *the memories* they made in that place," he corrects. "Memories created with people they love. As long as they've got the people, the place is just a place." He prowls out of view into the dining room.

I take a second, willing my pulse to slow down. Why am I allowing him free rein? It's that voice of his, I think. That intoxicating huskiness.

I round the fireplace from the other side and find him looking down at the beautiful bottles of skin care products on the dining table. Picking up one of the boxes, he reads it, then gives me yet another glower.

"You don't need this stuff," he says with a note of disgust. "You're the hottest woman I've ever seen."

My brain skids to a halt, even as my heart rate kicks up another notch. I'm speechless at the compliment he tossed out as casually as flicking ash off the tip of a cigarette. Composing myself, I focus on the other part of his comment. "I helped formulate those."

"Really?" Interest piqued, he takes a closer look. "How does that work? The formulating, I mean."

Cautiously, I move closer. "I take what I know as a cosmetic surgeon—the treatments and techniques, the outcomes patients are happiest with, the most popular areas of focus—and work with a team of scientists to design the optimal combination of ingredients to deliver visible results."

"Ah." He turns the box around, reading the text.

"All good stuff," I say, realizing I want him to be impressed. "We made it our mission to use sustainable, organic materials with a minimum of preservatives and no synthetic or artificial ingredients."

Garrett's head lifts, and his attention centers on me again. I feel the intensity of his gaze, feel exposed by it.

"Where's your office? Seattle? Tacoma?"

"Neither. I sold my practice when I moved here. Now I just focus on development of ECRA+ products, which means a lot of telecommuting and the occasional trip to New York."

"You're not doing that reality show anymore?"

I shake my head. "Technically, it's on an extended hiatus, but the producers are starting to make noise, and I'm not ready to go back, so . . ."

Those soul-searching eyes skim over my face. He sets the box down, rounds the table, and heads toward me. I move toward the door, hoping I can show him out. It's become overwhelming, having him in my home.

He pauses a few feet from me, glancing down the stairs that lead to the daylight basement. Then he passes right by me, heading into the hallway.

"Excuse me." I hurry after him but not fast enough to stop him from entering my bedroom. "You're crossing a line now, Garrett."

Ignoring me, he rakes the room in a single sweeping glance. Then he reaches into the walk-in closet and flicks on the light.

My arms cross over my chest. "What the fuck are you doing?"

The entire master bedroom feels like a closet with him in it. And our proximity to my bed puts me on edge.

Flipping off the light, he faces me. "Just making sure there's no other guy in my way."

My chin lifts. "Not that it matters."

He flashes that smile. I stand there stupidly, knocked completely off-center. That simple curving of the lips is even more charismatic up close, softening his rough edges. He reminds me of dreams I once had that are gone now, a bittersweet insight that makes my heart hurt.

"It would matter to me," he says.

He steps closer; I take a quick step back. He holds his hand out as if I'm a skittish animal. "Let's go out on the deck."

He edges around me, definitely cautious. His gaze stays on me as mine stays on him, my body turning so that he's never behind me. He reaches for the handle to the sliding glass door, unlocking it and sliding it open. The rush of ocean air fills my lungs and cools my heated face.

Garrett slides the screen open and steps out, moving over to the railing. I follow, feeling less constricted the moment the screen shuts behind me and we're both fully outside.

I join him at the railing, positioning myself a couple of feet away. Even at that distance, I'm hyperaware of him. Of how big and powerful his body is, how focused he is on me.

I'm hyperaware of everything, I realize with a jolt. The blue of the sky, the green of my lawn, the sounds of the birds, the tang of salt in the air.

"I wasn't expecting to ever feel this way again, Teagan," he says. "It's intense for me. You're telling me to ignore it, but I can't. And if you're being honest, you'll admit you can't, either."

His candor strips me of any weapons or defense. "I was doing fine before you got here."

"I don't think so." Garrett turns away from the view to face me directly. "This place doesn't have a single personal photograph of friends or family or even places you've been. Everything hanging on your walls was chosen to suit the house, not your soul."

"You don't know that."

"Yes, I do." He takes another step closer. We're toe-to-toe now, combat boots to Converse. His fingers entwine with mine. His body emanates heat, promising warmth after long months in the cold. "You've got a half dozen prescription bottles on your nightstand."

I stiffen. "You're going too far, Garrett."

"I just want you to know that I see you."

"Then you see a hot mess."

"Hey, I'm fucked up, too. But we still somehow ended up right here, feeling a spark that gave me a good reason to get out of bed this morning. Some things work out when you just let them be what they are. Let's try that for a bit and see what happens."

My mind scrolls through a million ways Garrett can send my life careering sideways. "I don't know how to do that."

"Sure you do." His head lowers. "Kiss me."

"That's a bad idea, Frost. I'm not like the house next door, you know. You don't get to take things that are off the market simply because you want to."

"So what are you saying?" He cups my cheek, his thumb brushing over my cheekbone. "You want to stand out here, look over at my deck, and see me with someone else?"

I turn my head away, trying not to picture it. "Can't you just move?"

Garrett laughs and pulls me into a hug. "I'm not going to take the lack of jealousy personally. And no, Doc, I'm not moving. I like living next door. Right where I can see you every day."

My arms go around his waist before I can stop myself, my hands caressing him through the soft material of his T-shirt. He draws me closer.

It feels so good to be held. To be touched and desired.

I'm going to give in. I want to blame it on him. He's too good at seduction and too used to getting his way.

But the truth is that when I'm with him, I don't feel so tired or lonely.

Tilting my head back, I offer him my mouth.

He shakes his head. "Not this time. I'm not sweeping you off your feet again. You've got to come to me of your own free will."

I don't argue or complain, not even to myself. Instead, I slide a hand around the back of his neck, tug his head down, and press my lips to his.

With a growl, Garrett takes over, his mouth opening, his tongue stroking. He winds my long braid tightly around his hand, easing my head back so that I'm arched over his forearm, taken and possessed. It's impossibly erotic, the way he savors me, the sense that he's parched for the taste of me. It turns me on to be caught by him, the power of his grip revealing how much I'm affecting him.

Heat rushes through my veins. My heart pumps faster, sending blood rushing to my head. I sway, feeling dizzy. Garrett shifts, lets go of my braid, scooping me up like a new bride. Flushed and vulnerable, I press my face against his chest, taking a deep breath of his scent.

I feel the flex of his arm as the sliding screen is pushed aside. In seconds, the bed is against my back, cushioning me as he settles his weight over me.

Being in my bedroom changes everything. I'm no longer shy. Anchored by a firmly planted forearm, Garrett knees my legs apart and notches the hard length of his erection against my sex. With a practiced roll of his hips, he has me moaning shamelessly into his kiss.

Pulling back, he watches me when he thrusts again, sees me tense and arch as shocking pleasure spreads through me. I embrace my wantonness, my hips rocking up against the tempting ridge of his cock.

"Teagan." He says my name in a voice hoarse with desire. "You're driving me crazy."

He rears back onto his knees, bringing me up with him. Switching our places, Garrett settles against my headboard, stretched out between my legs like some great lounging beast. His hands cup my thighs, sliding upward until his thumbs graze the place that aches for him.

I grab his wrists, afraid I'll lose all control.

"You can have it," he tells me, "but I want to watch you take it."

There's no judgment in his expression. No taunting. No triumph. As flushed as he is, as feverish as his gaze is as he watches me, there is patience and acceptance underlying the demand he conveys. And his face . . . that work of art. I see the cracks in the beauty, as if his perfect mask has slipped, revealing something unguarded and agonized and even more beautiful beneath.

I suddenly feel like crying.

"Hey," he murmurs. "Come here."

Shaking my head, I resist the comfort he offers, knowing how dangerous it is to become dependent on anyone but myself. Instead, I press my sex against his cock and begin to move.

Defiant, I hold his gaze as I swivel my hips, knowing I have a sensory advantage here. He's wearing denim. I'm wearing joggers and "invisible" panties of hardly any material at all.

"God, you're beautiful," he groans, his neck arching as I ride his erection.

It doesn't take long. The sight of him splayed for the taking, the smell of his heated skin, the encouraging sounds he makes . . . it's all too much. I gasp when the first intensely erotic spasm racks my core, my head falling forward as the incredible sensation spreads to my limbs. Quivering violently, I feel my rhythm falter.

Garrett rolls, taking me under him. Spreading his thighs wide, he begins to thrust, forcing the spreading orgasm through me, making me take it. His chest heaves as he dry fucks me with ferocious precision, tightening his grip as I writhe.

"Fuck," he gasps harshly. "I can't . . . *Fuck.*"

He stiffens, his breath hissing out through clenched teeth. His hips jerk against mine, his tempo wavering. I realize he's coming, too. While fully dressed, boots digging into the white coverlet.

His head drops next to mine, his damp cheek pressed against my own. His breathing is harsh in my ear, his embrace too tight. As if I'm some sort of lifeline.

I don't know how to feel. How can it seem so intimate when we're fully clothed?

His big body shakes with laughter. "My God. That is *not* how I intended to show you what you've been missing."

It startles me to realize I'm smiling. And I'm so relaxed and warm. Boneless almost, all the knots in my shoulders and back melted away. "I got the gist of it."

Garrett lifts his head to look down at me, his hand coming up to brush stray strands of hair off my face. "I swear I didn't have a hair trigger like that even as a teenager."

"Of course not. Gorgeous guy like you? You smile, and panties get wet."

His face lights up. "Is that what happens when I smile at you?"

"*Pfft.* As if."

He gives me a quick, hard kiss on the mouth. "Got any condoms?"

The question throws me off. It's been a long time since I worried about prophylactics. "No."

He gifts me with that high-wattage smile. "Good. But we'll need to get some."

My brows lift. I try to sound nonchalant when I ask, "Studly guy like you doesn't have a condom in his pocket?"

"I wish." The twinkle in his eyes tells me he's well aware I'm fishing. "I don't even have any in my house or my car. But I'm going to fix that before you come over for dinner tonight."

"I don't think I said I was coming." I'm teasing and he knows it, but it's fun to play the game and keep things light after an experience that broke down a lot of barriers I'm used to hiding behind.

"Aww . . . don't be like that, Doc. I really want you there. I even picked up some sparkling apple cider for you."

I can't say why that makes me laugh. Maybe because sparkling cider is so often a children's drink.

"That sound." Garrett nuzzles his nose against mine. "You've got the best laugh."

I smile ruefully, knowing the guilt will come later. I haven't laughed in so long, and I can't look back to the times when I last did. It would hurt too much.

"You've got to let me make you dinner," he presses. "I can't give you an orgasm and not feed you."

"See?" I pout. "You're making up rules as you go again."

"I'm also making sushi."

"I love sushi." Then my eyes narrow. "Isn't that risky, though? Doing it yourself?"

"Doc, I buy sashimi-grade fish, I promise." His hair has fallen across his brow. There's still a flush to his cheeks and lips and a light in his stunning eyes. He looks younger, happier, even handsomer.

"Okay, okay." I heave an exaggerated sigh. "I guess I'll come over, then."

Garrett winks. "I knew you would."

6

"I completely forgot you have mile-long legs for someone so short," Roxy says from her seat in the aqua Bertoia Bird Chair in my bedroom. "One: you need to wear dresses more often. And two: you need to wear *that* dress tonight."

"I just don't know." I'm lamenting the fact that I'm completely out of touch with both my femininity and sexuality. "I don't want to be overdressed."

"I'll put on a dress, too, okay? Will that make it easier?"

"It'll help." I turn from side to side. Problem is, my everyday wear is comfortable but not exactly fashionable or even flattering, and the clothes I have for work aren't casual enough for dinner with friends at home.

I own *one* dress that could pass for casual. It's black with a sheer cherry-embroidered overlay atop an opaque black underskirt. The sheer black takes over from a sweetheart bodice, climbing up and over my shoulders, before dipping down my back in a deep V. When worn with a red or black blazer, it's modest. Alone, it's impossible to hide a bra, and I don't own any bras cute enough to be exposed. I could wear my hair down for cover, but I'm worried that would be letting too much down at once.

"That dress is it," Roxy insists. "I love the way it swings when you move."

I meet her gaze in the mirror.

She stands and walks over. "I'm glad you're giving Garrett another shot."

"It's not like he knows how to take no for an answer."

"Good for him. And for you, too." She smiles at my scowl. "Think of it this way: seeing you in this dress is going to throw him for a loop. He won't know what hit him."

"Gah. That makes me think it's the wrong thing to wear."

She wags a finger at me. "If you're not wearing that dress when I see you next, I'm going to tell him how you tortured yourself trying to dress up for him."

"Roxy! You're supposed to be on my side."

"Girl, I am. That's why I'm making sure you hang on to Mr. Hunkalicious next door." She starts walking out. "I've got to get ready myself. Don't wait for us. Head over now and have him to yourself for a bit."

"That's asking for trouble," I call after her.

"Ask away! And remember, I'll want all the details later."

I hear the front door close behind her. I stare at the mirror for another long minute, debating my options. I end up back in my closet, looking for shoes. In the end, I go with a pair of black ballet flats. I twist my hair up in a knot. I also decide against jewelry or makeup to avoid looking like I tried to impress him. Garrett's too confident. There's absolutely no need for further encouragement.

"Screw it." I leave my bedroom before I change my mind. I grab my keys, phone, and the bag I decided on earlier, then head out the front door. I lock the dead bolt behind me and arm the security system app as I walk over to Garrett's house.

I try to slow down when I realize I'm walking fast. Still, I get to his porch too soon. I avoid looking through the big arched window by the front door, in case he catches me doing it.

My foot taps after I ring the doorbell, my nerves taut. When the door swings open, I straighten and attempt a smile but feel like it freezes along with my brain at the sight of Garrett.

His hair is still wet from a shower. He's dressed in head-to-toe black: untucked Henley top and slacks. The color suits him, plays off his dark hair and highlights those golden-green eyes. He is devastatingly handsome. The force of his attractiveness hits me dead center of my chest. The air between us charges with electricity.

It's not until my gaze makes it back up to his handsome face that I realize he hasn't moved or said a word.

"Hi," I greet him.

"Hi yourself," he says gruffly, leaning casually against the doorjamb and letting his gaze roam my body from head to toe.

It's disconcerting to feel so exposed, so *seen*. I've managed to measure what I share and what I keep private. Garrett has irrevocably changed that. Moving forward, I'm going to remember him like this, as well as in my house and on the street where I live.

"I'm the luckiest, dumbest son of a bitch on earth."

Startled, I blink. "What?"

"Doc, you take a man's breath away." He gives me a big, slow grin. "I'm feeling pretty damn pleased with myself right now."

"Of course you are," I say dryly.

Laughing, Garrett straightens. "And I'm an ass for keeping you on the porch. Come in."

I walk past him, setting my bag on the console in the entryway. When I turn back to him, Garrett catches me deftly around the waist, pulling me in as his head lowers to mine. It's like a dance, the way he claims me for a kiss, leading me so effortlessly, it's as if I spun intentionally into the embrace.

Maybe I did.

A soft sigh escapes me the moment our lips meet; then my eyes drift shut as I open to him, my hands clutching his waistband and my head tilting back. With a subtle shift, he aligns us perfectly and settles in, his lips soft and cajoling, his tongue a velvet lash. He savors me with deep, slow licks, and my core tightens in appreciation. His hands slide from my shoulders down my back, caressing me. My body arches into his, silently asking for more.

It always stuns me how quickly and easily he inspires my lust. My thumbs curl into his waistband, my pulse leaping when he stiffens and groans into my mouth. His fingers circle my wrists and pull my hands free, spurring me to make a soft noise of protest.

Pulling back, he looks down at me with heavy-lidded eyes, the gold so bright it's like they glow from within.

"Careful," he warns, his voice husky. "The next time you make me come, I'm going to be inside you. Most important, it's going to last a hell of a lot longer. Maybe a couple of days."

"Days?" A shiver runs through me at the thought.

His gaze darkens. "Dare me to prove it."

"I . . . I just . . ." Unable to find words, I shrug helplessly.

He grabs my hand and gives it a gentle squeeze. "Can I get you something to drink?"

"No, I'm good. Uh, I brought something. For you and for the party."

"Oh?" His smile makes my heart flutter.

I reach into my bag and pull out the box inside. He takes it from me, noting the kanji characters on the exterior packaging.

When he opens it, his smile widens. "Thank you."

"You're welcome." The sake set features a serving vessel and four small cups made of black porcelain with pure-gold interiors. The modern lines struck me as both masculine and elegant. I reach back into the bag. "I also brought a bottle of sake, in case you don't have any. And I got you some arnica cream. It's a homeopathic remedy for muscle soreness and bruising, for those days when you overdo it."

Garrett tucks the sake into the crook of his arm and accepts the tube. He glances at it, grinning, then meets my gaze. The way he looks at me makes me shift on my feet. "You worry about me. I'm taking that as a good sign."

"Don't get cocky, Frost." I turn away from him to take in what he's done to the house.

"Not cocky. Just hopeful."

My steps take me into the living room, which boasts the sweeping view of Puget Sound that most of the neighborhood has . . . and the sapphire velvet sectional sofa of my dreams. "Oh!"

Garrett's voice drifts from the kitchen. "What?"

"It's the sofa I wanted!"

"Is that so? Well, now you know where to find it. We can also do more than sit on it."

I look at him through the pass-through. "Do you think of anything other than sex?"

"You'll have to forgive me." His gaze is on the food he's chopping, and his voice is anything but apologetic. "It's been a while, and you're sexy as hell."

I almost ask him how long it's been, but I stop myself. After all, it's none of my business and isn't relevant in any case.

Instead, I look around the rest of the room. Marge and Les had filled it with a motley assortment of furniture upholstered in gold-and-tan plaid that didn't quite match their beige love seat. Garrett, on the other hand, has the show-stopping sofa and not much else. The coffee table is a beat-up trunk. There are no end tables, no lamps, no rug. A large TV sits on a shagreen console angled in the corner.

But what really dominates the room—overshadowing even the sofa—is the painting on the wall. I stand in front of it, so moved by the sight of it that my throat tightens and my eyes sting. I suddenly understand what he meant about the art I chose to decorate my home with. The designer had suggested mostly white abstracts, with pops of color that are aesthetically pleasing and enhance my overall palette. But I don't *feel* anything when I look at any of it. It simply finishes the space.

The doorbell rings. I tear my gaze away from the painting, feeling unsettled, needing a few moments to compose myself before Roxy and Mike join us. I turn to face the view of the Sound.

I register the pleasure in all three voices as they greet each other. How strange it is to adjust to this blending of the old and the new. How quickly Garrett has made a place for himself here, so unexpectedly.

"There's the pretty lady," Mike says, the register of his voice telling me he's entered the room.

"And there's a pretty couch!" Roxy exclaims. I turn in time to see her settle gracefully onto it. She changed into a floor-length caftan in the colors of sunset and looks like a queen on a jeweled throne. "It's so comfortable, too."

Stepping into Mike's hug, I manage to smile at her over his shoulder by rising onto my tiptoes.

"Wow! Would you look at that." Mike releases me and goes to stand in front of the large canvas. "I saw a photo of this online, but it's really something in person."

Garrett stands on the other side of the pass-through, opening a bottle of wine. His gaze is on me, serious and intent.

Can he see what the painting has done to me? How emotional it has made me?

"Do you paint every day, Garrett?" Roxy asks.

"I used to. I started a new piece a couple of days ago, but it's been a year since I last felt inspired enough to work. I was beginning to think I'd lost the creative spark entirely."

"Like writer's block?" Mike queries, shoving one hand into the pocket of his jeans. "Painter's block?"

"Something like that." Garrett comes into the living room, carrying two glasses of red wine so dark it seems almost black.

"Creativity in general can become blocked," Roxy says, accepting the glass Garrett hands her with a smile of gratitude. "You've got to be in the right headspace to feel creative."

"That's very true," Garrett agrees.

"Well, as Roxy can tell you, I'm no expert on art," Mike says, studying the canvas, "but for what it's worth, I really like your stuff. I think it's cool how your paintings don't look like the photos that inspired them, but I can *feel* what you were feeling when you took the photo. If that makes sense. I never understood abstract art, but I can understand this."

"Thank you." Garrett's tone is sincere. "If you feel something looking at my work, that's a high compliment, and I'm happy to take it."

Mike's smile widens, and he visibly relaxes as he accepts his glass. I remind myself that Garrett is a rock star in certain circles, a great-looking guy with boundless talent. Thanks to his penchant for dating supermodels, he's been mentioned on tabloid shows and gossip blogs, sat front row at fashion weeks, and popped up on high-profile social media feeds. I don't see him as a celebrity, but I understand that Mike and Roxy do. And Garrett has put Mike at ease in a matter of moments.

"This one in particular," Mike goes on, "just blows my mind. I thought so even looking at it on my computer. There's so much energy in it. And . . . I don't know. Joy? It makes me feel good just looking at it."

I can tell Garrett is touched. So am I.

"I was thinking the same thing," Roxy says from her perch on the sofa. She sits where she was before, with her legs crossed and one arm draped over the back of the couch, looking perfectly at home. "It's a happy painting. And it reminds me of snow. What was the inspiration photo?"

"A pile of ski gloves on a table," Mike answers. "Can you believe it? To see that and then see *this*." He gestures with both arms wide toward the canvas.

Garrett returns to the pass-through and takes a long drink of his wine, nearly draining the glass. "That was my breakout piece," he says somberly, licking wine off his lower lip. "Prior to it, I was focused on still lifes. It was my wife who challenged me to try conveying emotion through paint, instead of painting objects and trying to make them resonate emotionally."

Roxy's brows shoot up. "Oh. I thought you were a bachelor. Not that I know very much about you, but nothing to the contrary came up when cyberstalking you—I'm harmless, I promise—so I guess I just assumed."

His faint smile quickly fades. "When things took off for me, my wife preferred to stay in the background, so I never discussed my personal life when interviewed."

"It's great you kept the painting for yourself and didn't end up selling it to someone," Mike says.

"I did sell it, actually. I had to buy it back, but the fact that I wanted it returned made the buyer even more determined to keep it. He tried to wring me dry."

Roxy nods. "I can understand having an attachment to a breakout piece. I kept the first bowl I made; I was so proud of it."

"That was a factor, certainly." Garrett walks over to where I stand by the windows. "But what makes that piece so special is what you can't see. Underneath the abstract on the surface is the original still life of my wife's and son's gloves. I was so frustrated with her when she told me what I didn't want to hear about my art, I covered over what was already there. I was trying to prove a point but proved hers instead."

"You have a son!" Roxy's face beams. "How old is he?"

Garrett takes a deep breath before answering. "David would have been seven this year."

Turning my head, I look up at him, and the familiar cold, hard knot tightens in my stomach. His hand rubs up and down my back, as if he's comforting me, when it's *his* face that is stark and pale.

The moment hardens in amber, forever preserved. Mike and Roxy have frozen in place, their faces showing shock and sorrow.

I slide my arm around Garrett's waist, trying to impart whatever comfort I can. I rest my cheek against his chest, feeling helpless.

"Oh, Garrett." Roxy winces. "I don't know what to say . . . I'm so sorry."

"So am I," he says, releasing the tension in his body with a deep exhalation. "I'm sorry every day. It's been fourteen months, three weeks, and four days, and it still sometimes feels like a nightmare I'm waiting to wake up from."

"I . . ." She looks at Mike helplessly.

"There's nothing to say, Roxanne," Garrett tells her gently. "Losing a child is a horrible, godawful thing."

"I'm sorry," Mike offers, his voice gruff. He looks everywhere but at Garrett when he takes a drink. "I can't even imagine."

"Don't try." Garrett presses his lips to the crown of my head. "Just hold on to the ones you love. Make time for them. Enjoy them."

There's a pervasive weight in the air, a chill despite the sunlight streaming in. Garrett glances down at me, and I see the deep well of his grief in his gaze.

He stands tall, shoulders squared, chin lifted. A shattered man using all his strength to hold himself together.

7

"You hardly ate anything." Garrett is walking me back to my house. He reaches for my hand, joining our fingers together. It's later tonight than the night before, late enough that it's truly dark out.

"I'm just not that hungry."

He doesn't ask why as we climb the short set of steps that connects his yard—which sits lower on the bluff—to mine. We walk around the retaining wall that affords me a flat lawn, then onto the pathway to the front door.

"You stopped talking after I mentioned David," he says quietly.

I sigh and squeeze his hand. "I'm sorry if it seemed that way."

"It didn't *seem* that way; that's what happened."

I almost want him to be angry with me so I can feel something other than terribly sad, but he's not. His tone is matter-of-fact, his grip on my hand easy and comfortable. "I'm sorry, Garrett."

"Stop apologizing. I'm just checking in with you, that's all. You've been somewhere else most of the night, and wherever that is, I want to be there, too."

"And how fucked up is that? It should be the reverse. I should be checking in with you." I shake my head, angry with myself for being worthless to him.

I pause before my front door. Reaching up, I cup his cheek in my hand. After a year of wandering around in the dark, I see him becoming such a light for me. I feel things for him I thought I'd never feel again. That's why I don't want to be a burden that holds him back. "You deserve someone who can be a comfort to you."

"You are." He pulls me into a loose embrace. "Having you beside me tonight—that was enough."

"I don't think so."

"You don't get to say what works for me, Teagan," he says with gentle firmness. "It made you sad hearing me talk about it. That's normal."

Normal. I had a normal life once. *I* was normal once, but that's behind me. Sadness is something *normal* people experience within a spectrum of emotions. For me, it's a crack that widens into a chasm that swallows me whole and takes days to climb out of.

"I'm so tired, Garrett," I say honestly. I'm so exhausted, my limbs feel leaden. Even breathing is an effort. "I'm still fighting jet lag, and it's been a long day."

His frown is fierce. "It doesn't feel right leaving you alone right now."

"Don't worry about me. Besides, you've got Roxy and Mike waiting."

He rests his forehead against mine with a sigh. "If I don't come back, they'll get the idea and leave."

I can feel myself swaying in his arms, like a reed under water. The surface is farther and farther away as I sink.

"I'm seriously going to pass out the moment my head hits the pillow," I tell him, my voice sounding far away to my own ears.

He releases me reluctantly, watches me as I open, then close the door in his face. My keys hit the floor. Turning the dead bolt is too much work. I long for the couch but force myself into the bedroom instead.

It's been some time since I felt this way, but I recognize the path. And the destination. Only the oblivion of sleep can comfort me now.

∼

A soft moan escapes me when I wake up enough to comprehend that someone's knocking on the front door. The sound is aggressive, impatient, accompanied by demanding rings of the doorbell.

Drifting back to consciousness feels like being pulled from the bottom of a lake. I'm buried in mud and silt, the heaviness slowly sliding off me as I'm reeled back up to the surface. I fight the pull, turning to my side and squeezing my eyes shut. I'm still so tired.

I sense the light of the sun. I didn't close the blinds. The brightness tells me nothing about the hour. The sun rises early in the summer.

Reaching behind me, I yank the coverlet over me, wrapping myself in a cocoon. The noise fades, and I fall back to sleep.

The irritating sound of rapping on glass pulls me back to consciousness. Curling into a tight ball, I ignore it. But the door to the deck slides open anyway. A breeze rushes in, carrying the cries of birds and the distant rumble of airplanes. Why is the door open? I struggle to remember.

"Teagan."

The sound of Garrett's voice brings tears to my eyes. The door seals shut. The room is enveloped in quiet once again. He tugs at the bedspread, gently uncurling my clutching fingers, undoing my efforts to hold on to it. In short order, it no longer covers me.

"Oh, Doc," he says quietly, heartache in his voice. A shoe drops, then another. The mattress depresses under his weight, and he crawls onto the bed behind me. He wraps around my back until we're fitted as tightly as matched spoons. His arm bands my waist; his lips press into my neck. Warmth settles into me. I sink back into obliviousness.

~

The need to pee finally forces me to rise. I rub at my puffy, crusty eyes before opening them, seeing a soft orange glow on the wall that tells me the sun has made its journey across the sky. In my stomach, the ball of ice sits like a stone, burning with cold.

How can something so solid feel like yawning, agonizing emptiness?

Kicking out my legs, I wince at the tightness in muscles cramping into one position for too long. The arm around my waist loosens, freeing me to sit up on the edge of the bed. I don't look at Garrett when I stand or when I walk to the bathroom and shut the door. I don't look in the mirror after I've relieved myself and wash my hands. But when I open the door again, Garrett's waiting there, standing beside the bed in black running shorts and socks.

I look beyond him to the sliding glass door, realizing I must have forgotten to lock it after he and I came in from the deck the day before.

That interlude seems like it happened ages ago.

My gaze returns to him. A frown draws his brows together, and his eyes have darkened to a deep emerald. He looks worried and pale, and concern for him penetrates the numbness engulfing me.

It hurts to take a breath. Still, I manage it. "I'm sorry."

He catches me close, hugging tightly. "The only thing you need to apologize for is not letting me stay with you last night. Damn it, Teagan. I know what depression looks like, what it feels like. You don't have to suffer alone."

It takes a long while before what he said actually pierces through the fog in my mind. Licking dry lips, I tell him, "I'm not okay."

He presses a kiss to my forehead. "I can see that."

"You're so much stronger than I am."

"So? Maybe I am. You're a damn sight smarter than me. Helluva lot prettier, too. That's called balance."

"Check your mirror, Frost."

"No false modesty here. I know I'm a good-looking guy— I've been taking advantage of that with hot chicks like you my whole life."

I would groan at that statement if I had the energy. "You're trying to distract me."

"Not a crime."

"I'm so tired." I yawn, weary beyond belief.

"I ordered food while you were in the bathroom. If you eat something, you can go back to sleep."

Against my better judgment, I burrow into him.

~

Garrett glowers and stubbornly holds the spoon to my lips. "Keep going. You're only halfway through."

"I'm full."

"No, you're not."

I open my mouth just because I don't want him to spill soup on me, not after I dragged myself through a shower at his insistence. The soup has cooled but is still lukewarm. I have no clue what it is, aside from some kind of broth.

"It doesn't taste like anything," I complain after swallowing.

We're sitting in the dining room eating delivered take-out. I'm at the head of the table with my back to the adjacent kitchen. He's sitting beside me with his back to the view. Now I'll never be able to look out from this vantage without picturing him here, bare-chested and backlit by the slowly setting sun.

"This happens to be a damn good chicken noodle soup," he retorts. "You're welcome to my sandwich, if you'd prefer that."

"I'm not hungry." I feel like crap and also guilty. He's got to be starving after a day without food, but he's making sure I eat first.

I open my mouth to tell him I'm not a child, but he shoves a spoonful of soup in before I can get a word out. I glare at him.

"There we go," he murmurs, dabbing at my chin with a napkin. "Starting to see some fire in those pretty brown eyes."

"I'm going to dump that soup on you."

The deep frown line between his brows softens. "Oh yeah? Think you can take me?"

The thought is absurd. He's six foot three and at least two hundred and twenty pounds. That makes him a foot taller and nearly a hundred pounds heavier than me. There was a time in my life when I'd taken care of myself, worked out, ate well. Now . . . well, I'm too thin, lack any muscle tone whatsoever, and probably couldn't take on a kitten in play mode.

Still. "You wield a paintbrush, hot guy. I wield a scalpel."

"Ooh, fighting words. I like 'em." He finally sets aside the plastic tub of soup. Then he grabs the armrests of my chair and drags me into the space between his spread legs. "Speaking of paintbrushes . . . I dreamed about you last night. I had drop cloths spread on the floor, you were stretched out naked on top of them, and I was driving you crazy running brushes all over your body."

I'm in no condition to appreciate his sexual fantasy.

"Nothing?" he queries.

"What can I say to that? You're going to a lot of trouble to get into my pants, but you're far too gorgeous to work this hard for sex with a head case."

"Wow, that was a mouthful." Despite his amusement, the shadows linger in his eyes. "For the record, I'm shooting for more than a single roll in the hay."

"What happened to taking things one day at a time? Focusing on right here and right now and all that?"

"Yeah, we shot past that." Garrett takes my hands in his. "Now it's us—you and me—and tomorrow, and the day after that, and the day after that."

I lean closer, holding his gaze with my own. "You deserve to be happier than this. Don't punish yourself with me."

He sighs. "Teagan, I don't know what you think I should be out there looking for, when I've got all the mystery of the deepest oceans sitting right here in front of me."

That stuns me into a moment of silence before I protest, "I'm no great mystery, Frost. There's no treasure to uncover. What you see is what there is."

"I'm a guy who finds the expedition itself more worthwhile than the treasure. One can last forever; the other is the end of the road."

His gaze is earnest and direct. My head lowers. I look at my hands in my lap.

"I have shit days, too, you know," he goes on. "Trust me on that."

"You're not taking me seriously."

"You're looking at it the wrong way." His grip tightens. "You're broken. I'm broken. We don't throw the pieces away. We fit them together until they make something new."

A picture forms in my mind, rising through the haze. "Like the mosaics Roxanne makes," I say quietly.

"Exactly."

"Roxy wears gloves so the jagged edges don't cut her fingers."

"We're not wearing gloves. We're digging in with our bare hands, and if we get cut, well . . . you're a surgeon. We'll fix it."

"That's mixing metaphor with reality," I point out dryly.

Garrett gives me a genuine smile. "Nah, that's mixing you and me, babe."

I'm giving up the fight. I'm too exhausted; he's too determined . . . and too tempting. If he wants to deal with my shit, I'm going to let him. In the past, it would take me days to get around to showering and eating after hitting bottom.

He makes things better.

I doubt my ability to do the same for him, which makes me feel selfish. But I can try. He deserves it.

"You ready to go back to bed?" he asks.

"Not until you eat your sandwich."

"You keeping me company?" He reaches over and brushes the damp hair away from my face.

Turning my head, I kiss his palm. "That's my plan."

8

I tell myself not to get too excited before the doorbell rings, but when it does, I have to consciously slow my steps so I don't reach the door too quickly. I've already disarmed the alarm. It takes only a second to disengage the dead bolt. I have come to anticipate the early-morning coffee break I share with Garrett, and when I open the door, I'm reminded of the reasons why.

"Good morning, Doc," he greets me, standing on my doorstep in black running shorts and shoes. He's got one hand on my doorframe, his sculpted body casually on display. I take my time staring, as if I haven't been treated to the same exceptional view every morning for the past week.

Of course, if he were only physically attractive, I would eventually come to take it for granted. It's the powerful sexual confidence he radiates that takes my desire for him to another level entirely.

"Good morning, Garrett." Pulling the door open, I step back to let him in. I take a deep breath as he passes me. He smells so good. Then I close the door slowly, maybe too slowly, alive with anticipation.

I've come to crave the sensation of his mouth on mine, the way he tastes and how I feel when he holds me. There is a yearning for him inside me, growing every day.

I turn to face him, and he pulls me in with that dancerlike grace, his head coming down to press a kiss to my lips. My eyes drift shut; my lips part to let him in.

There is magic in a man who knows how to kiss well, and Garrett is as much an artist in this as he is in his work. The pressure of his lips is perfect, firm enough to convey desire yet soft enough to show an awareness of my comfort. The deep licks of his tongue are smooth, slow, and rhythmic, teasing me with thoughts of a more intimate penetration; his arms around me are a gentle cage, dominant yet tender. Above anything else, I know he'll be in charge when I finally take him to bed, and I won't object to that at all.

When Garrett eventually pulls away, I'm hot all over. Need for him pulses between my legs, making me squeeze my thighs together. All I want right now is to lie beside him and kiss him for hours. Just the thought causes a constriction in my chest.

He lifts my hands to his pecs and presses my palms flat against the heat of his bare skin. His eyes drift shut as I caress him. My fingers sift through the dusting of hair on his chest before tracing the intricate lines of his tattoos. The design is a single massive piece, not random images, and similar on both arms, though not mirrored.

"Teagan." He says my name on a sigh.

I love the feel of hard muscle beneath warm flesh. As my fingers trace the ridges of his abs, my gaze follows. He's so aroused from the kiss and my touch. His cock is proudly erect, the wide head peeking out from the waistband of his shorts.

My mouth waters. The evidence of his size, the impressive thickness and length of his penis, makes me hot. As I watch, a thick bead of precum pools on the broad head.

"Teagan, if you keep staring at my dick like that, my patience is going to run out real quick. Are you ready for that?"

I swallow hard and tear my gaze away to look up at his face. There's a high flush on those sculpted cheekbones and a provocative fullness to his lips from the fervor of my kiss. He's even more gorgeous when lustful.

But I'm more intimidated. Because we don't talk about his past or mine. We don't talk about next week. We exist only in the now and tomorrow, right here. Yet there is a part of me that has come to depend on him being around for a long time, as far ahead as I can imagine, and that's a terrifyingly dangerous precipice to stand on.

So I shake my head, knowing we have steps to take between here and there. "I'm almost ready."

"*Almost* is a step in the right direction." Garrett presses a swift, hard kiss to my forehead and backs away, adjusting his shorts. "Let's discuss over coffee," he suggests, his voice still passion-gruff but free of frustration or irritation.

Looks like it's a good day for him. It always takes me a little while to figure out if his mood is up or down. Regardless, his greeting is the same, and his kiss is always ardent. It's only in the moments after we slide apart that I can gauge whether ghosts haunt him that day or if they've let him be.

We tell each other we're just starting the day together, but it's also touching base for both of us, checking in with one another to make sure we're both doing okay emotionally. He's melancholy and pensive sometimes, yes. But he hasn't yet been depressed to the point where I'd feel compelled to intervene the way he did with me.

I move to the kitchen, avoiding his eyes because there are tears in mine. I can't let them fall. Because I know that for all his outward strength, he could still shatter, yet he treats me as if I'm the one who could break.

I go through the motions of making him a cup of coffee, giving us both time to settle. He takes it black, so it's simple to prepare, but I put care into it anyway, warming the mug with hot water from the instant tap before I fill it.

"How's the painting coming along?" I ask, because I know his art is an important part of his life, and it can either be a wedge between us or something we share.

"I'm nearly done with it."

"Oh? That seems quick . . . ?" I shake my head. "What am I saying? I have no idea how long it takes to finish a painting."

He smiles when I hand him the coffee. He's on the other side of the quartz-topped island, and I'm sorry there's something between us. I'm sorry for so many things I don't say.

"It's come together a little quicker than some others, especially considering the size, but I'm inspired." His lips curve against the rim of his mug, and his eyes gleam with silent laughter. "I'm also relying on the work to keep me off your doorstep and my hands off you."

"Oh." I take a deep breath. I've been aware that a clock is ticking somewhere, counting down the moments before we reach a turning point. It's good to know the timeline isn't completely arbitrary, but I feel as if I've wasted the breathing room he's given me by not moving things forward in some way.

"You know, Teagan, you can always say no, and I'll keep on waiting. You're worth waiting for." His gaze is tender. "But I have to ask: Is there something I can do or say to make going to bed with me less . . . daunting?"

His insight astonishes me. "Do you read minds?"

"I'm just paying attention." He takes another sip, his throat working on a swallow.

I never realized how sexy attentiveness could be. Garrett notices everything, and he uses that information to try and build a bridge between us.

"This matters: you and me," he asserts. "I can't tell you how much I'm looking forward to getting *us* started. It's no secret how much I want to have sex with you. But more than that, I'm looking forward to what happens *after* I have sex with you. Small things, like drinking coffee without my shoes on because we've just rolled out of bed together, and bigger things, like moving this wall between us out of the way so you're not half–turned on and half–freaking out every time I kiss you."

With a sigh, I lean back against the sink.

Garrett stares at me, his face serious. "I don't want to take that step if it's going to fuck things up somehow. So you tell me what's holding you back, and I'll see if it's something I can smooth out."

My fingers curl around the lip of the countertop behind me, gripping tightly. "Roads aren't always smooth, Garrett. It's dealing with the bumps that worries me."

"If we keep talking to each other, we'll be fine."

"But we aren't really talking, are we?" I rejoin. "We're walking on eggshells instead."

"I'm ready to talk. Are you?"

"No."

He laughs, and it's a rich, smoky sound of delight. "What am I going to do with you?"

"No idea, but I know what *I'd* like to do with *you*." My arms cross over my chest. "I think we need to get out of this little bubble we've been dancing in. You know, let some air in."

"Sounding good so far. What's your plan?"

"Have you been downtown yet? To Pike Place Market specifically?"

His brows lift with interest. "Can't say that I have."

"Can I tear you away this afternoon and take you up there? We can shop for some tasty things to put together a charcuterie board, then come back here and watch a movie."

He sets his mug down, places his palms flat on the countertop, and leans across so that we're eye to eye. "Yes. Absolutely."

His enthusiasm makes me smile. "Okay."

"And just to be clear: you can pull me away from work any time you want. Don't ever feel like you can't. I know I made that mistake before, putting my art above everything else. My priorities were all wrong." His fingers stroke along my jaw. "I can't promise not to fuck up, but I can promise to learn and do better."

I set my hand over his, laying my cheek against his palm. "I can't say how much I can change. I've kind of . . . mapped a route, you know? I've told myself that sticking to it will keep me from getting lost."

"Don't look now," he whispers, "but I think you're already recalculating."

My mouth opens to dispute that, but he puts a finger to my lips, one eyebrow raised in silent challenge. "Coffee and kisses every morning," he points out. "We're going on a date later, which *you* invited *me* on. Deal with it, Doc. I'm just irresistible."

Dropping his hand, he grabs the mug and finishes off his coffee.

"Is that right?" I shoot back, enjoying his teasing. It makes me happy to see him happy. Just as it hurts me to see him hurting.

"All signs point that way." Garrett rounds the island and takes his cup to the sink. "When we watch that movie later, bet you won't be able to keep your hands to yourself."

"You're on. Twenty bucks."

"A thousand."

"What? That's crazy."

He sets the washed mug in the drain and faces me. "You stick to your twenty; I'll stick to my thousand."

"Forget crazy. That's cheating."

"I prefer to think of it as added incentive." Hooking an arm around my waist, he pulls me in for a smacking kiss. "I'm going to run off some sexual frustration now. I'll be back in a couple of hours. Come get me when you want me."

I wrap my arms around his waist. "Don't forget to stretch and warm up before you start sprinting up the hills."

He hoots, grinning. "Yep, you definitely veered off course at some point."

Garrett heads out the door.

I already miss his energy and warmth.

~

I stand in front of the mirror, biting my lip and shifting from one foot to the other. I can't decide if I should wear the clothes that were just delivered or stick with something already in my closet. I ordered a new top and shorts with one-hour delivery, but I can't decide how I feel about the resulting outfit.

On the app, the top looked like a boatneck hemmed to petite length. In reality, it's completely off the shoulder, and—thanks to the low rise of the denim shorts—my midriff is bared more than I expected. Still, the top has long sleeves, and the alternating pale- and dark-green-striped material is more cute than sexy.

It's the lack of a strapless bra that's really throwing me off. I don't own one, and since the top didn't look shoulder-baring on the app, I didn't think to buy one. Not that I'm busty enough to absolutely *need* one. It's just that nipples can advertise the lack of a bra as much as jiggling can.

And this makes twice that I've deliberately dressed up for Garrett and gone braless.

With a growl, I give up. "I'm wearing this," I tell my reflection. "It's not like I'm building false expectations. I'm going to end up in bed with him at some point no matter what."

It liberates me to admit that out loud. I sit at my vanity, pull open the drawer, and look at my sad collection of makeup:

tinted sunscreen, a tube of mascara, lip gloss, and an eyeliner pencil.

Fact is, I stopped caring what I look like a long time ago, and making an effort to be presentable is just that: effort. When I'd had my medical practice, I made sure to look as flawless as possible. How else could I expect my patients to trust my aesthetic sense? Those days are gone.

It amazes me that Garrett finds me so attractive. Still, I want to impress him, at least a little. Throw him for a loop, as Roxy so eloquently put it.

By the time I'm done, I've used all the steps of the ECRA+ system on my face and neck and applied the sunscreen, eyeliner, mascara, and gloss. I french braid my hair straight back to keep it out of my face.

I'm out the door and bouncing up the steps to his house before I can tweak my appearance any more. My well-worn Converse are a casual touch—I'm definitely not trying too hard in that department—and the new outfit inspires confidence. But it feels weird to have the wind on my shoulders and back. And undeniably sexy.

After ringing the doorbell, I try to stop hopping up and down. I shift the shopping tote I brought with me from one shoulder to the other, even though the only items inside it are my keys and phone. Garrett shouts at me to come in, so I open the door and enter. I'm walking toward the living room when he rounds the corner from the hallway, stopping me dead in my tracks.

I'm used to seeing him in black, but his T-shirt today is navy, which looks great against his tanned skin and tattoos. His jeans are a faded blue, and his black boots are a canvas for drops of paint.

I give him an appreciative whistle. The man is seriously, dazzlingly hot. I can grumble about it all I like, but he's got every reason to be as cocky as he is.

My smile fades when he keeps on walking toward me, his jaw set in a tight line and his gaze intensely focused. Like the first day he appeared in my neighborhood, he's on a collision course with me, and I take a step back instinctively, my pulse kicking into overdrive.

"Don't you dare move," he warns, his voice deep and throaty.

I'm in his arms a moment later, and his mouth is on mine. My tote hits the floor with a definitive *thud*. Garrett lifts me effortlessly, bringing me up to eye level. I wrap my legs around his waist, appreciating the leanness of his hips and the firmness of his ass. My arms twine around his shoulders as my head tilts to deepen the kiss. His warm hand slides up beneath the back of my shirt, making me squirm before I break the kiss with a breathless laugh.

"That tickles!"

Garrett's smile is indulgent. "Sorry."

"No, you're not."

"I really am. Unintentionally tickling you broke up the kiss before I managed to sneak-walk you to the bedroom. How about we ditch the city and hit the sheets instead?"

I laugh. "You have a one-track mind."

"Not my fault." He sets me down. "You damn near gave me a heart attack walking into my house looking like sex on legs."

"My goal was to avoid embarrassing you in public," I say wryly. "You shouldn't look so good. Or smell so good."

"Since I'm hoping to keep you on the hook, I think I'll continue maintaining myself and showering regularly." He looks me up and down. "Cold showers."

He sighs, then runs a hand through his hair. "Can I get you something to drink?"

"No, I'm good."

He smiles and collects my tote. "Let's go, then, Doc, and show each other off."

9

"Are you driving or am I?" Garrett asks as we head out his front door with our hands linked.

I can't describe how it feels to have his hand in mine. What a comfort it is to me.

"Um . . ." I smile sheepishly. "Maybe I should have mentioned that I don't have a car."

His brows lift. "Are you kidding?"

"What would a born and bred New Yorker do with a car?"

"Well, you're not in New York, are you? And there has to be a mega-shit-ton of New York drivers, or there wouldn't be so many cars in the city. Do you have a driver's license, at least?"

"Of course. Just because I don't own a car doesn't mean I'm not capable of driving one."

"How do you get around?"

I shrug. "Rideshare, if I have to go somewhere. But I can get ninety-nine-point-nine percent of whatever I want delivered, so . . ."

Shaking his head, Garrett leads me to the Range Rover. "That can't be cost-effective."

"Depends on the value you place on your time. Also, the cost of insurance, car payments, the possibility of getting in an accident or injured, the ecological footprint of manufacturing—"

"All right, all right. I get it." He opens the passenger door for me. "For future reference, I'm right here. If you need something, let's go get it."

I climb into the cab using the deployed footstep and settle in. Having an excuse to spend more time with Garrett is fine by me, but I can think of sexier activities than shopping.

I get a swift, hard kiss to the mouth; then he shuts the door, rounds the hood, and slides behind the wheel. Above us, a panoramic moonroof lets in the sun, and Garrett grabs a pair of black aviators out of the center console. When he pushes the ignition button, music blares, and he quickly lowers the volume.

Using voice command, he directs the navigation to take us to Pike Place Market. Once we're set, he turns the volume up, although not as loud as before.

"Can I?" I ask, gesturing at the touch screen.

"Help yourself." Looking over his shoulder, he reverses, then starts up the driveway.

I sync my phone to his system, then scroll through the podcasts until I find a true-crime series I've been interested in.

Garrett looks at me, but all I can see is my reflection in his shades.

"Is this okay?" I ask, showing him my screen so he can see what I've selected. "Or we can talk. It's just that . . . I don't listen to music much anymore."

Grabbing my hand, he lifts my knuckles to his lips. "Yes, it's okay."

∼

Okay lasts until we make it to Pike Place Fish Market, the famous stall where cheerfully efficient guys toss heavy fish to one another. Located under the iconic neon Public Market Center clock in the heart of the Market, the sidewalk in front boasts Rachel the Pig, a bronze statue of a piggy bank that is endlessly photographed, and crowds of hooting observers watching—and recording video of—the fish flying.

Garrett is carrying my tote, now much heavier thanks to a bottle of wine, *salumi*, nuts, dried fruit, tapenades, crackers, and cheese, all from wonderful DeLaurenti, and a caramel apple dipped in dark chocolate from Rocky Mountain Chocolate Factory.

I'd taken him by Pike Brewing Company, then through the Atrium, where he saw the wooden *Sasquatch* statue (whose genital bulge has been noticeably manhandled too often) and the giant metal squid statue hanging in the air above it. We strolled past shops featuring First Nation art, Mexican crafts, graphic T-shirts with silly slogans, Asian imports, pharmacies, and everything else imaginable.

Everything was still *okay* . . . until we stepped outside and got swallowed into the crowd.

I'm highly conscious of the laughing children climbing all over Rachel, their oblivious parents too focused on the fish sailing through the air. The noise is deafening, orders and prices being shouted over the buzz of loud conversations in a variety of languages. Someone nearby hasn't bathed in a while, and two men to my left seem perilously close to duking it out. When a mother brushes past me to retrieve her child, her voice shrill with impatience and irritation, I can't breathe, and my heart races. My throat is tight, my eyes burning with dryness.

I want to back away. A few steps and I would be out of the suffocating crowd.

But I stay for Garrett. I train my gaze straight ahead and tune out my surroundings, thinking about how I'm going to arrange the charcuterie board, how I'm going to slice the *salumi*, which cheese I'm going to suggest pairing with which—

"Teagan." Garrett's voice is laced with strain.

I realize, as I turn my head toward where he stands beside me, that my grip on his hand is both too tight and damp with perspiration. Horrified, I let go. But Garrett does not.

It's not until my gaze reaches his face that I understand *he's* gripping *me* that hard, and his taut face is pale. His gaze is on Rachel . . . and the multitude of children clinging to her.

"Hey." I turn my back to the crowd and wrap my arms around his waist. Since he doesn't release my hand, his arm becomes pinned at his lower back. "You okay?"

He nods, but his jaw is clenched tight.

"Dumb question," I mutter. "Of course you're not. Let's get out of here."

"No. You said there was more."

"We don't need to see more. You're the only thing I want to look at anyway."

That admission pulls his gaze to me.

In the mirrored reflection of his sunglasses, I glimpse the phantoms that haunt him. I slide my free hand beneath his T-shirt to caress his bare skin. "You feel feverish, and your heart rate is elevated. And for a guy as tan as you are, you're far too pale."

A child's high, piercing laugh rends the air, and he jolts violently.

Garrett curses. "Let's get away from this spot."

I worry that won't be enough—and seeing him falter has shaken what there was of my strength—but we step back until we're at the curb, centered where Pine turns onto Pike Place. There are people all around us. We become an island in the midst of a stream of people flowing in either direction.

"Let's head back to the parking garage," I offer. For me, going home sounds more appealing than going forward.

Bending, Garrett pulls me tight into an embrace. His cheek presses against mine, his low voice harsh against my ear. "It's hard for me . . . seeing people with their children. Especially when they're focused on the wrong things. I want to grab them and tell them to fucking appreciate what they have."

"Oh, Garrett." I want to cry, but I can't.

"And when it's the opposite and they're enjoying their kids, it's like a knife in the chest. And I wonder why I have to suffer like this. What did I do to deserve this kind of pain?"

My forehead drops to his chest. I hold him tighter. If only I could take away his pain . . . He feels so deeply. I know that from his work and his ability to voice his agony. "I'm so sorry."

Someone walks by and tells us to get a room, his laughter grating.

Garrett ignores him and holds on to me so tightly, even the breeze can't come between us. As the minutes pass, I feel his breathing even out. Beneath my cheek, his heartbeat begins to slow. It takes longer for me to realize that I've calmed down, too.

His hand finally relinquishes mine and slides up to cradle the back of my neck. "I'm sorry."

"For what? Don't apologize to me."

"Am I freaking you out?" he asks before pulling away to meet my gaze. He touches my cheek with his fingertips.

"This crowd was. You're fine."

He turns his head and takes in the length of the arcade, packed with tourists. There are florists and farmers, leather goods and spices, jewelry and art of all sorts left to see. Across the street is the original Starbucks, featuring the original logo and menu; Piroshky Piroshky, famous for their deliciously flaky pastries; and my favorite, Beecher's Handmade Cheese, where I'd planned to take Garrett to pick up the last item for my planned charcuterie board: the Flagship cheese I'd included in the gift basket I gave him when he first moved in.

"Let's just go home," I tell him fervently. "Why put ourselves through more if we don't have to?"

"Because we do have to." He looks back at me, his full lips twisted wryly. "Life goes on, and we're still living it." Stepping back, he slides his hand down my arm to cup my elbow. "Let's do this."

Another hand touches my shoulder, and I turn around, my heart leaping at the sight of the pretty blonde who's walked up behind me.

"Teagan! I thought that was you." Her words carry a hint of Central Europe, and her smile is girlishly charming. Her hair is like sunshine, and it hangs in a sleek curtain nearly to her waist. She's chic, sporting black boots cuffed in black fur that matches the fur on the vest she wears over a charcoal bodysuit.

"Zaneta." The sight of her makes me jittery. "Hi."

"You haven't come to see me in a while." She glances at Garrett, smiling as she notes his hand on me. "Didn't I say you would date again? I knew it would happen."

I'm embarrassed enough to skip the introductions.

"Do you . . ." I try to swallow, but my mouth is dry. "Do you have news?"

She reaches for my hand and gives it a squeeze. "We can't talk here. Come see me. Give me a call, and we'll make an appointment."

"Excuse me," Garrett says, draping a possessive arm across my shoulders. "Who are you?"

"Zaneta." She extends her hand. "I've known Teagan for a while now."

"How do you two know each other?" he asks as he shakes her hand.

Her head tilts as she looks at him thoughtfully, the long fall of her hair sliding over her shoulder. "Something big is coming up for you, something to do with your work. You should come see me, too."

I cringe as she digs into the Louis Vuitton tote hanging on her shoulder and pulls out a business card. She hands it to Garrett and looks back at me. "I have so much to tell you, Teagan."

"Can't you tell me now? Even a little bit?"

As Garrett's head lifts from reading, his fingers flex into my waist. "We're going to go our separate ways now, Zaneta. And we're not going to see you again. Ever."

"Garrett!" I look up at him and see icy fury.

Zaneta offers a tight smile. "You're a skeptic; I understand. But Teagan can tell you how helpful I can be."

"Lady, if you were capable of helping me," he says with marked disdain, "I would've gotten a heads-up fifteen months ago. As it is, I think you're a charlatan taking advantage of a vulnerable woman, and that pisses me off enough to lose my shit. You don't want me making trouble for you—trust me. So walk. The fuck. Away."

Her lips purse, her blue eyes going flat and hard. She glances at me. "You know where I am, Teagan, and you know I can help you."

"Don't contact us again," he calls after her.

She flips him the bird over her shoulder as she crosses the street. I'm torn between following her and staying with Garrett. It's crazy, and I know it, but if she has news . . .

"A *psychic*?" Garrett hisses. "Are you kidding me?"

"Don't." My shoulders hunch. "You shouldn't have talked to her like that."

"She's a fraud, for fuck's sake."

"So?"

103

"*So?* That's your answer? You *let* her fleece you out of God knows how much money?"

My foot taps against the curb. "I wasn't fleeced. And I can afford it, in any case."

"Damn it, it's not about the money, Teagan! It's about exploiting you."

"Don't judge me!" I turn on him. "I am so *tired* of being judged."

He crosses his arms over his chest, simultaneously defensive and aggressive. "I'm not judging you."

"Liar."

"Knock it off," he snaps. "I'm mad at her, not you."

I straighten to my full height. "You think I'm an idiot."

"I think you know better," he corrects tightly. "You're too smart to be swindled like this."

"So . . . what? I temporarily lost all reason and did something stupid? Is that what you're saying?"

He looks up at the sky; a muscle in his jaw tics visibly. "You're twisting things around."

"No, I'm clarifying." I walk away, needing to get far from the crowds, the noise, and the smells.

"Teagan! Don't walk away from me."

I speed-walk, darting around and among people, my smaller size making it easier for me to cut through the crowd than Garrett.

"Teagan, goddamn it!"

His voice is farther away, but I'm still picking up speed, amped on adrenaline and anger. I round the corner to Western and head to the parking garage. Garrett catches me by the elbow before I get there, pulling me around to face him.

How the hell can he look so damn hot when he's pissed off and I'm pissed off at him?

"Stop running," he snaps, even angrier than when he'd confronted Zaneta. "We're having a conversation. You don't get to walk away in the middle of it. You don't get to walk away *ever*. You got that? We're hashing shit out."

People pass by us, turning their heads to stare.

"I'm not running." My words are bit out, one by one. "I'm saving you the embarrassment of getting your ass chewed in public."

"What are you mad at me for? I haven't done anything but worry about you."

"Oh, you're wrong about that, Frost. Seriously wrong. The only person standing here who hasn't fucked up is me."

His frown turns thunderous. "You better start explaining yourself."

I give him a tight smile. "I can't wait. But we're getting in the car first."

10

Garrett starts walking, pulling me along with him. "You're using this as an excuse to get out of here, instead of sticking through and dealing."

"You really need to stop talking," I warn him.

We don't talk as we make our way to the Range Rover. Garrett opens the door for me, then puts the nearly full tote bag on the floor in the second row behind me. I soak in the brief quiet as he comes around to the driver's side door.

He hops in, turns the vehicle on, programs the navigation, then shoots me a look.

"When we get on the highway," I tell him.

Garrett sets his arm on the back of my seat and looks behind him as he backs out, muttering, "You try my patience, Teagan. You really do."

We make our way down one-way streets, then up startlingly steep streets rivaling San Francisco, and finally onto the freeway.

"Why don't you just talk to Roxy?" he asks as soon as he hits the on-ramp. "She's a good friend to you, isn't she? I know she's worried about you."

My spine goes rigid. "What did you tell her?"

"I didn't tell her anything." He glances at me. "She noticed all the security on your house, how strict you are about locking things up. She thinks maybe Kyler was abusive when he was using."

My ex-husband's name hangs heavily in the air for a moment.

I look out the window, watching the city passing by, not willing to waste words talking about my ex. "Have you heard from Roxy since the dinner at your place?"

"No. We've waved at each other now and then, though."

"She's avoiding you," I tell him flatly. "If she wasn't, she would have stopped over a couple of times by now. That would be her usual pattern. Plus, I'm sure she's dying to ask you questions about your work. She's an artist, too, after all. It's very out of character for her to stay away."

"What are you getting at? She doesn't like me?"

"She adores you. But thinking about David . . ." My fingers twine in my lap. "It's awkward for her, I'm sure. Pain, depression, grief—most people want to stay far away from those things and the people affected by them, even if they're otherwise great friends."

"You're saying I shouldn't have told her." His knuckles turn white on the steering wheel. "I can't pretend my son didn't exist, Teagan. That would feel like losing him all over again."

I sigh. "What I'm trying to say is that yes, Roxy is a good and caring friend, but people shy away from uncomfortable situations, and I can't afford to lose Roxy or Mike."

"So you talk to a psychic instead? Why not go to a therapist? Someone who can actually help."

"You have no idea how many times you've hurt me in the past hour," I say quietly. "Or that I'm about to scream, waiting for the next time you're going to hurt me again."

"Teagan." Garrett reaches over, setting his hand on my knee. His touch is warm and dry, meant only to be reassuring. But it sends a flare of sexual awareness through my whole body. "I never want to hurt you. I honestly have no idea what's going through your head right now. I need you to tell me."

"You say you're not judging me, but you are."

"That's not—"

"Let me finish. You could have asked why I went to see Zaneta. I knew she didn't have any real answers. I was aware every time she started fishing or made a prediction that was way off base or totally wrong. It didn't matter, because there were some days when I didn't see any point in being alive, and she gave me false hope, and sometimes that's better than no hope at all."

His fingers flex into the flesh of my thigh. "Okay, I get it. I—"

"No, you don't. You just presumed I'd have to be out of my mind to see her, instead of having made a conscious decision to do so. And you concluded I was throwing my money away without realizing it. But what really hurts is that you automatically default to thinking my way is wrong just because I handle things in a way you wouldn't."

This time, he doesn't try to speak over me.

"Just because I deal with my issues differently doesn't mean I'm not dealing with them the 'right' way."

His chest expands; then he exhales in a rush. "I didn't realize I was doing that. I'm sorry."

"You suggested I should've talked to a friend or a therapist instead, because that's what makes sense to *you*. But you know what, Garrett? Neither a friend nor a therapist would create a fantasy for me that gives me comfort, even if it's only temporary. I paid Zaneta for that, and as far as I'm concerned, she gave me what I paid for."

The freeway curves, and snowcapped Mount Rainier suddenly dominates the landscape.

Garrett's breath catches.

I, too, am awed by the mountain's enormity and the dichotomy of a bustling metropolis so near such an extraordinary geological feature. It amazes me that, more often than not, Mount Rainier is hidden behind fog and clouds. It seems impossible that something so majestic, so *colossal* can hide in plain sight. Maybe that's why I feel such an affinity to it.

"I'm sorry, Teagan. You're right; I was wrong." He glances at me. "But more than that, I learned something from this. I'm going to be more aware of how I react to things in the future."

I absorb his apology, taking a moment to admire his profile—the masculine line of his jaw, the strength of his neck. Then I look back at the mountain.

"If you keep talking," he goes on, "I'll keep learning, and we'll keep growing stronger."

I set my hand over his where it rests on my lap and squeeze.

The ride home is quiet but not uncomfortably so. Garrett's fingers are now linked with mine, his other hand resting easily on the wheel. The aviators shield his eyes from the sun, and I look over at him often.

I think of what he said earlier and take in the view of the mountain. There are stretches on the drive home where Mount Rainier is in the perfect position to be appreciated.

"I really love it here," I say aloud. "I think it's just beautiful."

He glances at me and smiles faintly. "There's definitely beauty here."

My lips twist wryly. "Not your best effort, Frost."

"I'm saving my really good lines for later." His brows waggle over the top of his sunglasses, and I laugh silently at the absurdity.

When we reach Garrett's house, he parks the SUV in front of the garage, then hops out to open my door. "Are we taking this to your house or mine?"

"I'm good with either."

The twinkle returns to his eyes. "I have the blue velvet couch."

My lips curve in spite of my lingering irritation. "Your place it is."

He heads back around to the driver's side, opens the door, and hits a button on the rearview mirror that opens the nearest garage door. My eyes widen as a multitude of fitness equipment comes into view. A stationary bike, a treadmill, a dumbbell rack, and a variety of weight machines fill the space designed for three cars.

As we walk through to the door leading into the house, I tell him, "I think I'm going to try out Roxy's gym."

"You're welcome to come here."

"Just the thought intimidates me." Once inside, I join him at the kitchen island. The cabinets throughout are white, except for the island, which has black cabinetry and is topped with black granite veined with gray. The countertops are so bare, it seems almost as if no one lives here. But there's a coffee maker by the sink and a professional set of knives.

Then I spot the wicker basket I gave him on another counter and the loaf of bread sticking out of it. My heart warms at the sight.

"What intimidates you? The equipment? Or me? I can stay out of your way if it's me," he offers.

"Both, actually. And I lack your discipline. Roxy says her gym has small classes and is heart rate–based, so you always know if you're working too hard or not hard enough."

"Interval training, right?" He turns to put some of the food we bought into the fridge.

"Yes. Do you want me to put the board together now? Are you hungry?"

"I'm always hungry. How about you?"

"Yes."

Garrett turns back and sets the stuff—wrapped mortadella and some cheese—back on the island. "How about I slice what there is to slice and you arrange?"

"Deal."

He holds my gaze. "And how about I drive you to the gym and join with you?"

"Really? But you've got all this stuff here."

"Doesn't mean I can't enjoy getting sweaty with you."

I smile. "Okay."

He washes his hands at the sink. "Glasses are in the cupboard to the left of the fridge. There's juice, water, iced tea. Or I can make you something hot?"

"I'll get it, thank you."

He sets to work as I pour myself a glass of iced tea. I realize, as he starts unwrapping what we bought, that there's a lot to do.

"Can I help?" I ask.

"Nah. I got this."

"Should I go get my charcuterie board from next door?"

"I have one."

"Really?"

Looking up, he winks at me. "Really."

"Makes me wonder what else you've got around here that would surprise me."

"I'm full of surprises, babe." He pulls a wicked-looking knife out of the block on the counter and starts slicing into a log of salami.

And I admit he's not wrong—he's been surprising me since the day he showed up. "Do you mind if I look around?"

"I didn't ask you when I went through your place."

"I have better manners."

He grins. "Be my guest. I keep my boxer briefs in the top drawer on the right, in case you want to snag a pair to put under your pillow."

"Where do you come up with this stuff, Frost?" I move toward the hallway.

"Teagan."

The gravity in his voice has me looking back over my shoulder. "Yes?"

Garrett sets down the knife, his face austere. "There are family photos in my office. I closed the door before you came over, but you're welcome to go in there. If you want to. It's the only door that's closed."

I take that in, then nod slowly. "Thank you."

He manages a grim smile, then goes back to work.

I head down the hall. The first door I pass was Les and Marge's guest room, which seems to be the one he's using. I inhale deeply, smelling him. This door was closed the night he had us over for dinner, and I wondered then what he was using it for.

A large platform bed covered in gray sheets and comforter dominates the room. There's a dresser across from the foot of the bed and a single nightstand closest to the door. There is no hardware on the natural wood furniture, which boasts clean modern lines, and the large window is bare of any covering, providing an all-encompassing view of Puget Sound.

One of his paintings hangs on the wall, this one a misty blend of crimson shades that vaguely suggests the lines of a woman's nude body. It's smaller than the piece in the living room and, unlike that one, overtly sensual. I feel flushed just looking at it. Turning away, I see his running shoes in the corner. On top of the dresser is a shiny black dish holding a single ring: a gold band.

My heart is hurting when I leave the room, the echoes of love lost resonating deep.

The guest bathroom is next, and it's evident Garrett uses it as his personal washroom. It was cleaned up during the dinner party, but now the glass-enclosed shower holds his razor and toiletries. I've long admired the washroom's Calacatta marble vanity and shower, as well as the brass fixtures that add warmth to the space. I somehow like it more now, with all his personal items scattered around it.

I also can't help but picture him in that big standing shower, all that deeply tanned and tattooed skin, those rippling muscles, that impressive penis . . .

Clearing my throat, I quickly flick off the light and back out to the hallway.

The next door is closed. I pause in front of it, debating the wisdom of looking inside. I'm not sure I want to see the man he was before, when I'm just getting to know the man he is now. I'm afraid I will compare the two and that could somehow disrupt the tenuous bond forming between us.

Still, my fingers wrap around the door lever. I hold it long enough to warm the brushed nickel. Then I hear a soft noise and look down the hall, finding Garrett leaning into the wall, watching me. We stare at each other for a long moment. His face gives nothing away. As charming as he is when smiling, he's truly beautiful now, so quiet and serious.

My hand falls back to my side. I think he sighs, but I might have imagined it.

"Can I go upstairs?" I ask.

"Of course."

I turn left to climb the staircase, knowing the entire top floor is the master bedroom despite never actually seeing it before. The staircase curves, and light floods the way in front of me. A breeze drifts through, bringing the scent of fresh paint to my nose. There's a small landing at the top of the stairs, but it's empty. Straight ahead, the double-door entrance to the room is wide open, exposing a view of the Sound very much like the one in my living room, which is level with his second story.

It's obvious the master bedroom is his workshop and used for nothing else. There is a mini fridge in the corner, topped with a microwave, which in turn is topped by a hot plate and teakettle. The hardwood floor has been completely covered with canvas drop cloths, underneath which I can spot newsprint taped wall-to-wall. Aluminum ladders of varying heights stand open or lean, folded, against the walls amid scattered cans of paint. There are brushes of all sizes and shapes, some new in their packages, others laid to dry on an industrial workbench after cleaning.

A quick look into the outsize master bath shows a double-sink vanity with dozens of mason jars holding more brushes.

I deliberately avoid taking in the painting Garrett's working on until there's nothing else I can look at. When I finally focus my attention on it, all I can do is gasp.

11

"Do you like it?"

Spellbound by the violent beauty of the work, I don't turn at the sound of Garrett's voice. While still an abstract piece, it's far removed in tone and style from his other paintings. "It's . . . I don't have the words. *Beautiful* seems too tame. It feels like it's *moving*."

And it looks like the abyss I've spent so much time in over the past year. It's like he saw into my mind and gave it visual life.

The giant canvas soars toward the high, pitched roof and is covered in varying shades of white, gray, and black, from the lightest fog to the darkest ebony. The brushstrokes and shifts of color give the impression of both a whirlpool and whirlwind, with the luminescence of light in water and the misty edges of a rain-lashed tornado. In the eye of the storm, a sinuous ribbon of bright white highlights the maelstrom, gliding up as a thin line at the bottom and broadening at the top. Pale pink edges the white as it grows in prominence, creating a point of serenity and beauty in the midst of the tempest.

"It's gorgeous, Garrett. It . . . moves me." Reaching out, I trace the band of rosy white without directly touching the canvas.

"That light in the darkness is you," he says quietly, coming up behind me and wrapping his arms around my waist. "The rest is me."

Tears sting my eyes. Armed with that insight, I can see that the furious storm is less about rage and more about agony. The depth of his anguish wounds me deeply. The thought of him working on this for the past several days, putting his soul into it brushstroke by brushstroke, makes me so sad.

I lean into him, feeling his warmth at my back and his strength supporting me. "I feel the same," I tell him softly, "in reverse."

His lips curve in a smile against the bare skin of my shoulder before he presses a kiss there. "Totally what I was going for," he teases.

And just like that, the sadness dissipates. That's his magic. It awes me to think I might wield that same power over him.

His hands slip under the hem of my top and splay across my belly.

"I want to buy it," I say abruptly, unable to imagine anyone else having it.

"It's not for sale."

"Garrett!"

"Sorry, Doc. Not everything I create is for public consumption. Some things are just for me. But you can always come over and look at it."

I pout. Tingles are spreading across my skin from the rhythmic glide of his fingers along the lower curve of my breasts. My nipples have tightened into hard points, shamelessly begging to be touched. Or sucked.

His lips brush against my ear. "I'm just as hard as you are."

I pull in a shaky breath.

Garrett's hands finally cup my breasts, his thumbs and forefingers wrapping around the aching tips and rolling them gently.

My head falls back against his shoulder, a low moan filling the air between us. I can feel his erection cradled between the cheeks of my buttocks.

"You ready for what's next?" he asks, his voice husky.

Turning, I face him. His eyes are dark, his cheeks flushed. His lips part, the tip of his tongue gliding along the seam. There is so much about his face that I love.

"Yes," I answer without hesitation.

"Come on, then." He holds his hand out to me and leads me back downstairs.

I'm unaccountably nervous, my breathing too quick. "Should we put the food away?"

"Already done."

"Was this a foregone conclusion, then?"

"I'm an optimist when it comes to you, Teagan." We enter his bedroom, and my pulse races. He faces me. "I need you more than I need anything else. I'd even give up painting for you, if that's what it takes."

Amazement replaces my nervousness. "I would never ask you to do that."

"I hope you don't, but I wasn't painting without you and don't expect I could if I lost you, so"—he pulls his shirt over his head, tossing it aside—"if I ever have to choose between the two, I choose you."

He sits on the edge of the bed and bends to untie his boots, as if he hasn't just declared a level of affection and commitment that will forever change both our lives. I'm shaken, achingly aware that what's about to happen next has become more than a "next step." And I'm okay with that. More than okay. But . . .

I point at the painting on the wall. "I don't know if I can give you what inspired that."

He doesn't even look, his gaze on me instead. "I'm not looking for what I had. I'm too busy wanting what I have in front of me right now."

I toe off my Converse and reach for my liner socks.

"Just the socks and shoes," he tells me. "I'll take care of the rest myself."

"Then I get to take off your pants. And briefs."

He grins wolfishly. "Deal."

The other boot hits the floor and is tossed in the corner with the first one. His socks come next. He folds them together, then tosses them aside, too. The entire process is somehow erotic. The beautifully defined lines of his back as he bends over, the way his abs flex as he straightens, the bunching and releasing of his biceps.

"You are seriously hot," I tell him. "And very, very sexy."

Garrett stands and towers over me. "I'm very glad to hear that killing myself to impress you was worth the effort."

"Oh God. Don't even."

"No lie." His hands grip my waist. "I've been trying for every advantage I can think of."

"Which puts me at a total disadvantage," I whisper.

His hands grip the hem of my shirt and tug gently. "Let's even things up a bit."

Taking a deep breath, I stretch my arms over my head. The top lifts and blocks my vision for a moment, which only makes the change in Garrett's breathing more noticeable.

When I see his face again, his eyes are a bright gold.

"Now I'm the one who has no words," he says gruffly.

I reach for the fly of his jeans, my fingers trembling as I work to free the button. His erection is hard and thick behind the denim, straining against my knuckles.

"I'm nervous, too," he tells me.

Shaking my head, disbelieving that statement, I manage to pop the button through the hole, then catch the zipper pull in my trembling fingers. The placket falls open, revealing boxer briefs and a prominent bulge stretching against the black fabric.

Garrett lifts me, then sits on the edge of the bed, pulling me onto his lap so I straddle his hips. His chest is hot against my bare breasts, the light dusting of hair teasing my nipples. He smells wonderful, just a trace of citrusy musk that is both refreshing and stimulating.

"No fair," I complain. "We had a deal."

"I know, and we'll get there, I promise. I'm just a little too excited right now, and I don't want to go too fast."

I pout. He smiles, then grips me by the nape, pulling me in for a kiss. It starts out slow, with teasing licks of his tongue between my lips.

His mouth . . . God, it's truly divine. He holds me in place as he ravages me with a skilled, possessive kiss. My hands run up his chest and over his shoulders, kneading the hard muscle, caressing the firm skin. My palms tingle with the contact, sending frissons of electricity along my arms.

I moan his name. My hips rock against him, desperate to find friction.

Garrett twists at the waist, holding me to him as he lowers me to the bed. I try to wrap my legs around his hips, but he slides away, his lips circling my aching nipple with drenching heat.

I gasp and arch upward. Laying his forearm across my chest, he holds me down. He sucks rhythmically on the tender point, his tongue flickering over the taut peak with wicked precision. My core tightens greedily; my clit throbs with jealousy.

Panting, I dig into the mattress with my heels. "Garrett, please."

His mouth moves to my other breast, drawing with hot, firm suction. The breast he abandoned is cupped in his hand, plumped with soft squeezes, his thumb brushing over the cooled wet nipple.

Tilting my hips, I rub against the ridges of his abs, moaning as the erotic pressure makes my core tighten like a fist. His lips slide between my breasts, his tongue stroking a line down my stomach to my navel. He circles it with his tongue, dipping in, then gliding lower.

I'm certain I'll combust if he doesn't let up. I want to tell him to slow down, to let me catch my breath, regain control. The words won't form; the thought goes unsaid.

I reach for his shoulders, but he rises, tugging open the button fly of my shorts before yanking them off me in one powerful movement.

When my bare bottom touches the coverlet, I realize he's completely undressed me. There's nothing to hold him back now, and he proves it, sliding his hands behind my knees and pushing my thighs to my chest. He dives between my legs with a groan that flows over me in a rush of goose bumps.

I cry out when his tongue slides through the folds of my cleft, the tip seeking and caressing my clit. Hairless and smooth, my most sensitive flesh has nothing to blunt the stroke of his tongue. I moan, shuddering softly when his tongue flutters over the tender opening to my sex.

Arching my neck, my eyes squeeze shut. My thighs fall open. My fingers push into his hair, feeling damp heat at the roots.

Garrett grips the back of my thighs, holding me open to his questing mouth. His lips circle my clit, forming a tight ring through which he sucks. A long, breathless cry escapes me. Perspiration blooms over my skin in a mist of heat. The teasing tugs make my core clench in rhythmic need, desperate to be stretched and filled.

His hands slide down until his thumbs caress the lips of my cleft. He pulls me open, exposing everything. As his head lifts to look at me, my hands cover my face.

"I can't wait to slide into you," he says, lusty smoke in his voice. His thumb pushes through sensitive tissues. He groans when I tighten helplessly around the shallow penetration. "You're so tight and wet."

Swallowing hard, I touch his cheek. "Now. Do it now."

Withdrawing, he licks the pad of his thumb, tasting me. "I'm fucking you with my tongue first," he growls. "You're so damn sweet, I might eat you for hours."

I make a sound of protest, reaching for him, but his hair is too short to pull. I can only watch as Garrett lowers his dark head, his tongue licking his lips before his mouth is on me again. A slow, tormenting swipe through my cleft, then his talented tongue is thrusting inside me, stroking with ruthless skill.

My back arches off the bed, my body racked by sharp pulses of pleasure. My core tightens in mindless hunger, wanting everything he's got to give me. Deeper, harder. The heat of Garrett's palms covers my breasts, squeezing the swollen flesh, spurring need to tear through me. His tongue plunges in and out, taunting with the promise of a deeper, more thorough fucking to come.

"Garrett, *please*." I don't care if I'm begging. I can't lie still. I feel like I'm crawling out of my skin, lost to an animal hunger that makes embarrassment or modesty impossible.

He tugs my nipples with the gentle pinch of his fingers; then his splayed hands slide over my belly and his thumbs find my clit, pressing and circling. The orgasm tears through me, stiffening my spine even as my sex spasms around his thrusting tongue. He groans against me as I come for him, the vibration of the sound spurring a second wave of climax. Cupping my hips, he lifts me, eating my pussy with lush, voracious licking.

Black spots swim before my eyes. I take a deep breath only to arch violently again, driven to yet another orgasm by hot, wet suction on my hypersensitive clit.

It's too much; I can't bear it. I have been numb for too long. The rush of sensation is painfully acute. My heart feels as if it's pounding against my rib cage, my lungs burn with the need for air, my skin feels as if it's being assailed with a million pins and needles.

"Stop," I gasp, my hands fisted in my hair. "God, please *stop*."

Garrett sets me down and pulls away, his labored breathing harsh in the near silence. Sweat slides down my throat and between my breasts. I lay sprawled, panting, my sex throbbing. It takes all my energy to curl into a ball. I have denied myself pleasure for so long, a prohibition Garrett shattered with ruthless, passionate determination.

He shoves his jeans and briefs down his long powerful legs, kicking them aside. My gaze drops between his thighs, a soft whimper escaping me. He is so hard and ready, his penis curving up from the wide root to the broad head that reaches for his navel. A slick bead of precum runs down the side of the thick shaft, following the line of a thick, prominent vein.

Yanking open the bedside drawer, Garrett grabs a condom and rolls it on. There is a determined slant to his jaw, his gaze feverish. He's holding on by a thread and about to let go.

Oversensitized and overwhelmed, I roll onto my stomach and crawl toward the other side of the bed, my tumbled hair drifting all around me. I feel the mattress dip under his weight; then his hand wraps around my ankle, staying me. I tense, afraid I won't survive his unleashed lust. Then my head bows, my entire body softening in supplication. That simple touch, the small connection between my skin and his palm, is enough to soothe me.

My elbows bend, lowering my chest and shoulders to the comforter, my ass lifted. Garrett's hand slides up my thigh to my hip; the other steadies me by the waist.

"You okay?" he asks, with that jazz-bar voice that is a seduction in and of itself.

I nod, my eyes closing. I widen the spread of my knees.

His lips press against my lower back; then his hands grip the front of my thighs above the knees and gently pull my legs flat on the bed. He stretches out alongside me, one heavy arm across my back, one leg over both of mine. His hot, damp cheek is against my shoulder. His cock prods my hip, eager and insistent.

He hugs me like that for long moments, his chest heaving, his body trembling.

Confused, I query, "Garrett?"

"There's no obligation, Teagan," he says hoarsely. "I can wait."

"What?" I wiggle away enough to turn my head toward him. We lie face-to-face. The gold is gone from his eyes. "I'm ready. I just needed a minute."

His gaze is desolate in its lack of light. "I can't risk fucking this up. As much as I want you, it's not worth losing you."

I touch his face, running my fingertips over his brow. "Garrett. I want you. I do. It was just a lot, you know. *You're* a lot. I had to calm down a little."

When he doesn't move or speak, I twist to lie on my side. His leg slides away to free me of its weight, but I follow, hooking my knee over his waist and tugging, pulling our hips closer.

He eyes me warily, his big body straining with the need to rut. Every ridge and valley of his torso glistens with sweat. His penis stands proudly, defiantly erect between us.

I want it. I want him.

"You told me once I could have it," I remind him, "if you could watch me take it."

He doesn't move, aside from the heavy lift and fall of his chest. Then the tense muscles of his torso ease visibly, and the bleakness in his eyes softens into something tender and hopeful.

Garrett reaches between my spread legs, his fingers sliding gently through my slick cleft.

A shiver racks my body. "I'm too sensitive," I whisper.

"Just need to know you're ready."

"I've never been this ready."

He manages a strained smile, his hand retreating to rest on my hip. The smile disappears the second I take him in my hand, stroking from base to tip with the circle of my fingers.

A low moan rumbles from his chest. "Teagan," he gasps. "I can't . . ."

I slide closer, stretching my arm pinned between us up and over my head to pillow my cheek. He does the same, his fingers linking with mine. With my other hand, I pull the rigid length of his penis away from his abdomen, positioning him to fill me. Despite his warning, I stroke the flared crest of his cock through my cleft, my eyes half-closed with drugging pleasure.

Garrett's head falls back, his jaw clenched. His muscular legs quiver. His grip on my hand is painful, but I don't complain.

I notch the broad tip of him into the opening he ravished with his tongue and push my hips forward. The feel of the wide head pushing through my tender, swollen tissues spreads heat through my veins. I rock my hips, working that big shaft deeper. Intoxicated by the feel of him, by his utter stillness as I use his body, I run my hand over his chest, finding and teasing the flat disks of his nipples. My hips swirl, my body moving in a sinuous dance, my sex gliding onto and off his stiff cock, taking more with every push of my hips.

The sharp sound of rending fabric startles me. Garrett's other hand is behind him, gripping the comforter. Sweat slides down his torso, pools in his navel. I can hear his teeth grind as my sex ripples around him. I am impossibly turned on by the way he watches me and the ferocity of his gaze, which promises equal retribution for the sensual torture I'm inflicting now. He's literally ripping things apart with his need to take over, but he holds out, waiting for me.

Biting my lower lip, I return his stare. I want to tell him so many things. I want to share how I feel, how grateful I am that he showed up on my doorstep. But now is not the time, and my throat is too tight to speak.

So I nod.

With a growl, Garrett slings his arm around my back and twists, taking me under him in one effortless movement. He plants the hand gripping mine into the bed, the other cupping my buttock to angle me the way he wants. His knees dig in. He pulls free in a fluid withdrawal and thrusts hard, tunneling in to the root. I cry out, my back arching.

Head bowed, he pants, his hips grinding mindlessly, screwing his cock deep. "Sorry."

I clasp his hips with my thighs. "Stop being sorry and fuck me."

His gaze meets mine, the gold bursting through the green. He retreats, then slides deep, gentler this time, more precise. My sex tightens in delight, delicate nerves stroked to pleasure. His body heats instantly, his flesh blazing against mine. The scent of his skin intensifies, awakening something primal and possessive inside me.

Watching me, Garrett moves, swiveling his hips as he plunges inside. I'm compelled to writhe by the way he stretches me, the powerfully sensual feeling of fullness. Sweat drips from him to my chest.

"You feel so good." His voice is leaden with pleasure. "You're squeezing me so tight."

I lick dry lips. "Faster. Harder."

"I want it to last." He pulls back, thrusts. Withdraws, plunges deep. The rhythmic pumping, unhurried and adept, stokes a fire in my blood.

Tightening my legs around his hips, I spur him on, lifting into his leisurely drives. The tension builds, rippling through my sex, milking his shaft. He curses, his pace quickening.

My neck arches. I'm no longer capable of rational thought, my entire being centered on the wet, hot slide of his cock between my thighs. "You're so deep . . . Garrett. So hard and thick . . . Make me come."

He breaks then, his hands curving under my shoulder blades to hold me as he starts fucking in smooth, powerful drives. I'm coming before I can take a deep breath, the building pressure in my core releasing in a rush. Groaning, Garrett powers through the rippling waves of my orgasm, his body shaking as the climax takes him.

My nails dig into his waist; harsh cries rip from my dry throat. Hips churning, he pulls me tighter into him, careful to support his weight on his forearms. I hold him, my lips moving across his cheek.

I taste the salt of his sweat. Then his cheek presses against mine, and I realize it's tears.

12

"We're so classy," I tease Garrett as we both sit naked with our legs crossed on the blue velvet sofa, wrapped in throw blankets and eating a hastily compiled charcuterie board with our bare hands.

"I'm fucking starving," he mumbles around a bite of cheese, finishing it fast. He's looking too handsome for words, his short hair an adorable mess. He reaches for a slice of prosciutto, and the throw slips off his broad shoulders to pool in his lap. His bare torso is a work of art.

Behind him, the sky is a rainbow of pinks and oranges, the sun still making its leisurely dip toward the horizon. I want to take a picture of him like this. I want to preserve this moment forever.

"We can order something for delivery," I suggest.

He wipes his mouth with the back of his hand, straightening. "Do you want something else? I can cook."

"Nope, I'm good."

"I can make some spaghetti Bolognese. Or ramen—the real deal, not the packaged shit. I can whip up breakfast, too. Eggs, bacon, pancakes."

I smile. "This right here is fine with me. Really."

He studies me. "You sure?"

"I picked out all this stuff, didn't I?" I gesture at the board, then roll up a slice of mortadella with pistachio nuts and nibble on it. "I only suggested takeout because I'm worried it's not enough food for you."

I know that maintaining that ripped body of his requires plenty of fuel.

He grins at me. "You fuss over me, Doc. I like it. I like it a lot."

I snag a piece of spicy *soppressata* and sandwich it between a folded slice of provolone. "Where's your camera?"

"In my office. Why?"

The mention of his office, which brings to mind the photos inside it, stiffens my spine. I shake my head. "Never mind."

"Why'd you ask?"

"I just wanted to take a picture of you right now, the way you are. A good one, not one on my phone."

Because this moment we are sharing is a step away from reality, a magical time when we see only the best in each other and avoid acknowledging anything negative. I want to capture a small piece of this honeymoon period while I can. Because the bad times *will* come, and, as much as I hope for the best, I expect the worst.

Garrett shoots me a measured look from beneath those ridiculously thick lashes. "Want me to get it?"

I shake my head and stretch my legs out to stand. "No, stay just like that. If you get up, you'll blow the shot."

His gaze lifts to follow me as I rise. "You going to get it?"

I look toward the hallway, thinking, pulling the throw tighter around me. So much has changed over the course of the day. I've changed. *We* have changed. But some things are very much the same.

"It's a problematic shot anyway," he murmurs, chewing on a bite of salami. "The light is behind me."

I understand he's giving me an out. But a man who makes his living through photographs will own a camera that can make any shot work, even without ideal lighting. I look at him. "Do *you* want me to get it?"

Licking his fingers, Garrett studies me. "I want you to spend the night. I don't have anything more ambitious on the agenda."

Absorbing that, I nod. "Okay."

I pad in bare feet over to the console by the front door and collect my phone. Returning to the couch, I open my camera app, swipe over to the low-light setting, and snap the picture.

"Well?" he queries, popping an olive in his mouth.

I turn the screen to face him, smiling.

He raises his brows. "Not bad."

"Not as great as the flesh-and-blood version, but it'll have to do."

Leaning forward, he offers me his mouth. "The flesh-and-blood version's right here, babe," he murmurs into the kiss. "And not going anywhere."

It feels naughty putting on the same clothes I wore the day before when I get out of the shower. I look in the mirror as I twist my damp hair up into a knot. My lips are plump and red, my eyes rimmed with shadows. There's a dull ache of exhaustion throughout my body and other aches of a more intimate nature. It's barely nine in the morning, and I'm already contemplating a nap. Garrett, however, is ready to work.

"Here you go," he says, filling the doorway to the bathroom and holding out a mug of steaming coffee. He's dressed in worn jeans with random paint splatters. The best descriptor for him right now is scruffy, which is a sensational look on him, of course.

"Thank you." I know from the sight and smell of the coffee that it's been prepared just the way I like it. Taking a sip, I give a little moan of delight.

Garrett stares at me. "You can't make that noise around me."

My mouth curves. "Why not?"

"You know why not. My dick's now hard enough to drive nails."

I look for proof. "That's impressive."

"I'm glad you think so." He leans his shoulder into the doorjamb. "You're coming right back?"

"Oh, I don't know about that." I take another sip. "I figured I'd let you get to work, and I'll go walk the dogs with Roxy. Maybe take a nap. Maybe get some work done myself."

"I'll take a nap with you."

I arch a brow. "I think we've already established that you and I together in the same bed doesn't equal sleep."

"Just letting off some steam." He gives me a slow smile. "I can behave."

Garrett's extremely healthy sex drive has been on my mind all morning. How long has he gone without? Or maybe he hasn't. Maybe I'm the latest in a long string. I tell myself I have no right to care either way or to read anything into it.

"What's wrong?" he asks, straightening.

Damn if the man isn't too perceptive. An inevitable side effect of how intensely he pays attention to me. I'm still trying to adjust to that. I am used to being an afterthought.

I manage a smile. "Nothing."

"That means something."

"Not always. Sometimes nothing is nothing." I change the subject. "Would you like to go out to dinner tonight?"

"I'll go anywhere with you."

His eagerness to please makes me uneasy. He can't set aside his own wants and needs to accommodate what he thinks *I* want. That strategy isn't sustainable for the long haul.

"If you get busy or inspired or . . . whatever—just let me know," I tell him, aware that after the way I responded when he missed dinner at Roxy and Mike's, he's going to be hesitant about canceling anything. "I promise I won't be upset if you just let me know it's not a good time to break away."

He steps closer, taking up all the space in the bathroom. "I'm always inspired by you. You're my muse."

My heart gives a little flip, but I try to play it off. "And here I thought you were just using me for sex, but even your ulterior motives have motives."

"If I've got a need, Teagan—you fill it." He wraps his arms around my waist. "And I'm determined to make that work both ways. I'm going to become necessary to you; that's my plan."

I set my mug on the vanity and search his face. When his fingertips run over my cheeks, I close my eyes.

"Have I told you how much I love your freckles?" he asks. "I'm glad you don't cover them up."

"There are too many to even try."

Garrett kisses the tip of my nose, then reaches down to cup my rear. "I love your ass, too."

My gaze narrows. "Asians aren't known for their curves, and I'm no exception."

"You're half-Asian and all perfect, including this." He gives my buttocks a squeeze.

"You're just buttering me up so you can get to work," I say dryly.

"Not true, although I do have something new in mind I want to get started." His eyes light up thinking about it.

"Well then, don't let me hold you back."

"To the contrary." Garrett's smile is a thing of beauty. "You set me free."

Garrett walks me back to my house, despite my protests.

"If you decide to snooze," he says, following me inside, "I want to know about it."

"I'll consider it."

"Teagan." He says my name with a teasing note of warning. "If you end up sitting around, come back over."

"Go away now, Frost." I toss my keys on the end table. "You have things to do."

"Sure." He grins. "You're one of them."

"You're ridiculous."

"That's the way you like me." He catches me up and kisses my neck.

I place my palms on his bare chest. "Let's just plan on dinner, okay? Seven o'clock? We can head down to Salty's at six, and you can have a drink or two at the bar before we eat."

His playfulness turns into contemplation. "What happens when you drink?"

"I cry. A lot."

"Is that a bad thing?"

Inhaling deeply, I open up a little. "Life, for me, is like trying to breathe underwater most days. Adding tears makes it feel like I'm drowning."

"Ah, babe." Garrett presses a kiss to my forehead. "I won't let you drown. I promise."

My hands curl into fists against his skin. He doesn't understand that when you crack something open and everything spills out, you've got nothing left but a shell.

I kiss his chest, then slide my arms around him, giving him a quick hug. "You go get to work."

He frowns. "I always hate leaving you. It never feels right."

"Hey." I smile. "I'm not going anywhere, either."

"I'm holding you to that."

He lets me go and reaches for the doorknob behind him. Pulling the door open, Garrett reveals Roxy standing there, with her finger on the doorbell.

"Good morning, Roxanne," he greets her.

She stares for a moment, which I certainly can't fault her for. He is shirtless, after all.

Her hand lowers back to her side. "Garrett, good morning. How are you?"

The moment she asks the question, she winces.

He steps back to let her in, then switches places with her to move outside. "You showed up just in time. I do the gentlemanly thing and walk a girl home and end up getting groped, kissed—"

"Garrett!" I protest, trying not to laugh.

"I'd tell you all about how I suffer as the object of her lurid sexual fantasies," he goes on, backing away. "But I'd be lying, 'cause I like it."

"Shut up!" I take a step to go after him.

He winks at Roxy, then meets my gaze. "Don't miss me too much, Doc."

Garrett heads back to his place as I join a laughing Roxy at the door.

"Don't trip over your ego!" I yell after him.

Roxy puts a hand on my shoulder. "He's too much."

"Too confident."

"So gorgeous."

"Way too sexy," I continue. "And stubborn as a mule."

"Just what you need."

"Ha! Thanks." Shutting the door, I turn to find Roxy giving me a once-over.

"You look great," she tells me. "I love that top."

"Thank you. But since this is now a walk-of-shame outfit, I'm going to change real quick. Give me a minute."

"I am so proud of you right now!" she calls after me. "No wonder he was looking so damn pleased with himself."

"Don't encourage him!" I tug off the top and wiggle out of the shorts, tossing them both in the hamper. I pull a pair of joggers off the shelf, a T-shirt off a hanger, and dress quickly.

When I walk back out to the living room, I find Roxy making herself a cup of coffee. She gazes down at the filling mug when she says, "I have to talk to you."

"Okay."

She looks over at me. "About Garrett."

I nod. "That's what I figured."

"Did you?" She heaves a sigh, then turns to the fridge. She's wearing navy capris today and a V-neck top with white and gray stripes. As usual, she's accessorized beautifully with gold bangles on her wrists, large gold balls dangling from her ears, and pale-gold slip-ons.

"You haven't reached out to him since he had you over for dinner," I point out.

Turning away from the fridge with a container of half-and-half in her hand, Roxy looks crestfallen. "Did he say something?"

"No. I don't think he actually noticed until I pointed it out, and even then, he wasn't concerned. Maybe eventually it'll bother him, if you don't work it out."

She sighs again.

"Right now, he's okay," I go on. "But I'm not."

13

"Teagan. I'm sorry. I really am."

Joining Roxy at the counter, I pull a mug out of the cabinet and make myself a cup of coffee, too. She puts away the half-and-half, then returns to me with the almond-milk creamer.

I no longer feel the anger and disappointment I felt yesterday. Today, I just feel resigned yet hopeful. It's a brutally sad fact that a number of people simply disappear from your life when you're broken and need them the most. I'm counting on Roxy to be one who hangs tough.

She takes a seat at the dining table. "I never realized I had it in me to be a coward, but thinking about what happened to Garrett breaks my heart. His pain makes me feel . . . uncomfortable. I mean, what if I try to say something and it's the wrong thing to say?"

I search for advice, attempting to put into words what I wish more people had done for me when I began spiraling.

She waves her hand at the door. "I can't believe I just asked him how he's doing. What kind of question is that to ask someone going through what he is?"

I want to hug her for being that aware.

"He didn't seem to mind at all," I point out. "Everyone asks that question. It's like talking about the weather. Don't beat yourself up over it."

"I have no point of reference for this," Roxy says, her fingertips tracing the nautical design that wraps her mug. "I don't have kids; I've never lost a pet. My parents, grandparents, siblings, and in-laws are all alive and kicking. What do I know about losing someone you love?"

"You know enough to be concerned and cautious." And I'm so filled with relief, I feel light-headed. Knowing her heart is in the right place means everything to me. Sometimes people give what they can, and it's important to acknowledge that, even if it's not what you need.

"That's not enough," she gripes. "I mean, you're dating the guy! And you're my friend. I want to know the man in your life. I want us to all hang out together."

"So let's hang out together," I say with a shrug. "I wasn't there when you guys had wine together the other night, but you all seemed to really hit it off. Can't you go back to that?"

She looks at me miserably. "How? Then, he was just the new hot, rich, famous guy in the neighborhood making moves on my friend. Now, he's the tragic artist who lost his family. The look on his face when he talked about his son . . ." A shudder moves through her. "It was awful."

I remember that haunted look well and how deeply it cut me, too. "I know."

Her shoulders hunch. "Garrett's wonderful. He really is. I like him a lot. I've got to get over myself and reach out to him somehow, before he thinks I don't like him."

"When he's standing in front of you, I don't think it'll be as hard as you think. He's very charming."

"He is." Roxy takes a sip of her coffee, then puts the mug back down. "Do *you* ever feel awkward about it?"

I hesitate. Then, "No. Although I understand why you'd feel that way. Grief is such a personal thing, isn't it? And once you know that someone's suffering all the time, it's always in the back of your mind when you talk to them."

"Which means it's got to be on his mind, too."

"I'm sure it's something he lives with every day." I look out the windows at the Sound. "I can see it in his eyes when he's thinking about it."

"How can you stand it?"

"Because I'm beginning to realize that being with him is a lot better than being without him." I lean heavily into the seat back and get to the point. "I need you to be his friend, Roxy. It's important to me."

"I want to be. I just feel so . . . helpless." Wrapping her hands around her mug, she blows a quick breath through the steam. "How do you handle it when he talks about it?"

"We haven't."

Her eyes widen. "At all?"

"No. We're just . . . I don't know. Being very cautious." I look out the windows again. "The sexual attraction took us both by surprise, I think. Me more so than him, maybe. The minute he understood it was mutual, he was ready to jump in. I was warier. I don't have a great track record with relationships, as you've mentioned before."

She smiles then. "He told us you ding-dong ditched him and left a basket of goodies."

"I did." I return her smile. "I pictured him living on Cup Noodles and wading through boxes. Boy, was I wrong."

"Yeah. It looks like he's been living there for years, not weeks. The man does have it together, doesn't he?"

"Exactly. Which is why he's not going to break down on you. He gets quiet sometimes when he comes over for coffee, and he had a rough moment when he and I were downtown, but he copes and moves forward."

"Maybe you're helping with that," she suggests gently.

I sigh. "I wish I could, but we're two very different people that way. I'm far more private. I compartmentalize well—I've been told *too* well—and he . . . connects. He shares. He talks. I see those differences becoming a problem eventually. He thinks we'll work it out."

"I hope you do." She straightens in her seat. "I'm going to order some books, I think. Someone's got to have written something about helping friends grieve."

"Roxanne." I swallow back tears, but they still fill my eyes. "You're an amazing woman."

"Don't go all watery on me. You know how I get."

Her mock-stern tone makes me smile. "We're going to Salty's for dinner. You and Mike are welcome to join us."

"Oh, I don't want to intrude on your date."

"You wouldn't be. Besides, you know you want that seafood chowder."

Her eyes light up. "With a splash of cream sherry and fresh cracked black pepper. Lord, is that good."

"Especially when you dip that fresh hot buttered bread into it . . ."

"Okay, fine. We'll come." Reaching over, she grips my hand. "Thank you."

"For what? I haven't even gotten to the part where I invite you to come with me when Eva Cross visits Seattle."

"Wait. What?" Roxy's on her feet, gaping down at me. "Are you kidding?"

"I wouldn't dare. You'd kill me."

She nearly bounces on her feet. "Is she really coming here?"

"Yes. They're rolling out ECRA+ skin care through the spas in Cross hotels. She's got press interviews scheduled to promote the planned pop-up at Cross Towers here in Seattle, and while they're at it, they want to get new photos of me for their promotional materials."

Dropping back into her seat, she leans forward. "Okay. Give me all the details so I can figure out what to wear. Date. Time. What everyone else will be wearing." She mulls it over. "I'll have to buy something new."

I take a sip of my coffee and hide a smile behind the rim of my mug. There are many obstacles ahead, so I'm going to enjoy smooth sailing while it lasts.

∼

"God, Teagan." Garrett's hands pull on my hair. "Your mouth . . ."

I grip his cock in both hands, stroking up from the root to where my lips are wrapped around the wide crest. Hollowing my cheeks, I suck hard, then flutter my tongue over the tip.

My entire morning has been spent thinking of him this way, my mind wandering from the emails I need to answer to thoughts of Garrett at work in his studio. I pictured him in his jeans and bare feet, imagined going to him, opening his fly, and taking his cock in my mouth.

In the past week since we first made our new relationship sexual, we'd done a lot of things to each other, but giving him a happy ending blow job hadn't happened yet. Finally, I just couldn't wait anymore. I came to his house, climbed the stairs, and took what I hungered for.

Garrett's hands fall to either side of his hips, fisting the drop cloth beneath him. "Oh fuck, that's good."

My tongue circles the flared head, my eyes on him as he writhes with pleasure. I'm so turned on by the sight of his big body straining beneath my touch, every muscle hard and flexing under damp skin. Kneeling between his spread thighs, I feel the slick heat of arousal coating my sex.

White-knuckled, Garrett holds on as I tuck him against the roof of my mouth and suck rhythmically. He's so close, I can taste it, his cock head creamy with excitement. I cup his tightened scrotum in one hand, feeling how firm his testicles are, how high they've drawn in anticipation of orgasm.

I release the pressure, sliding my lips up and off so I can lick down the length of the rigid shaft, tracing the thick prominent veins that lay sinuously between the wide base and broad crown. His hips lift beneath me, the instinct to thrust too strong for him to deny.

"Suck me," he growls. "Put that hot mouth on my dick and suck me 'til I come."

The words are harsh, as is his voice, but his hands remain where they are, the lust violent but the man still gentle.

Warmth suffuses my chest, my heart aching with emotions I never thought I'd feel again.

Licking the taste of him off my lips, I pull him into my mouth again. I suck in earnest, my head bobbing, my hands milking the cum from his heavy sac.

"It's so fucking good." His hand returns to my hair, holding me still. His hips rise from the floor, pumping his cock through my lips.

Palms down on the drop cloth, I hold myself steady as he begins to fuck my mouth with steady, shallow upward drives.

"I'm going to come," he bites out. "I'm going to come so fucking hard."

Garrett's back stiffens, his cock jerking before a burst of semen spurts on my tongue. With his hips raised high and his body shuddering, he climaxes for long moments, filling my mouth as I work to swallow.

Gasping, he finally sinks to the floor, tremors racking his body. I pull air into my lungs in deep gulps, settling back on my heels with my hands on my thighs.

"Teagan." Garrett's growl of my name is the only warning I have before he rises, catching me up and rolling me to the floor on my back.

He shoves my legs to my chest, yanks the waistband of my joggers and underwear up to my knees and out of the way, then thrusts his still-hard cock inside me. I cry out, startled and so turned on by his forcefulness, I'm a stroke or two away from coming.

Bent in half, my knees by my ear, my legs restrained by my pants, I have no leverage to participate. I can only lie there as Garrett rides me hard, thrusting his big penis into my desperately slick sex. Tension builds in my core, my breaths coming in sharp pants of pleasure. When the orgasm hits, it's like a rolling wave, breaking in a rush, then lapping against my senses in a series of deep, slow pulses.

He waits until the last tremor is a memory, then withdraws wetly, sliding free in a heavy glide. I roll to my side, feeling as if all my muscles have weakened, my pants and underwear still tangled around my calves. Garrett collapses on the floor beside me, curling into my back and tossing an arm around my waist. His chest expands and contracts against me like a bellows, his breathing harsh but slowing.

"That one's going in the hall of fame," he says hoarsely. "I think I may actually have died when you sucked me off, and the rest was part of my afterlife."

I laugh; I can't help it.

He lifts his head and plants a firm, quick kiss on my cheek. "I need to know what set you off so I can make it happen again."

Reaching down, I attempt to tug on my clothes. It strikes me then that he was naked when he fucked me, but I'm still mostly dressed. I find that very erotic.

"It just seemed like a good idea," I tell him, rolling to my back and hoisting my hips to wriggle into my pants.

"It was an excellent idea." He pushes up onto one elbow and rests his head in his hand. The other comes to rest on my tummy. "Let's do it again. In New York."

My head turns toward him. "What?"

"I've got an exhibition next week. I left a lot of pieces in the city when I moved here, and we're working on selling them off." He runs the tip of his finger down the bridge of my nose. "I want you with me."

I release my breath slowly, considering the request. It would be a big change for us if I accompanied him, and I worry about making any drastic shifts in our budding relationship. Still, the thought of days without seeing him makes me anxious. "When do you have to go?"

"I'm thinking I'll fly out Tuesday, meet with the gallery owner on Wednesday. The opening is Thursday. There will be an after-party, but from then on, we can do whatever we want. We can spend the weekend in the city and fly back Monday."

My brows lift. "This coming Tuesday?"

"Yeah. My agent's been after me for weeks to get out there, but you and I were just getting started, and that was my priority. Most everything was easily handled with video and email anyway, and my social media team has been handling the promotion side of things, so it's all good."

With that admission, how can I say no? But I have to. "I wish I could, Garrett. I really do. And normally, I'd be able to. But I've already agreed to appear at an ECRA+ promotion in Seattle this Thursday, and I promised Roxy I would introduce her to Eva Cross—she's a huge fan. Mike says she's been driving him nuts getting ready for it."

He frowns. I can hear him thinking.

"Okay . . ." Rubbing his jaw with one hand, he says, "I'll switch it to a video appearance at the gallery. I've done it before; it's easy."

"Absolutely not. It's a big deal—I know that. Even if you've done dozens of openings and exhibitions, every one of them is a big deal, and you should be there. I'm not holding you back."

His jaw sets stubbornly. "We already talked about this. My priorities are different now."

I sit up and cross my legs. "I get that. And I appreciate it—I really do. But I shouldn't come first *all* the time. Just most of the time."

I try to make that into a joke with a bright smile, but Garrett is scowling when he sits up, brazenly naked.

"I'm not screwing this up," he says tightly. "You and me. Us."

"You will, though, if you don't go to New York."

The scowl turns into a glare. "How so?"

"Because shorting your career for me will never work in the long run, Garrett."

"One time won't hurt anything," he protests.

"That's how it starts."

Garrett's eyes take on a stubborn glint. "You're the most important thing in my life. I don't want to do anything that makes you doubt it."

The relationship battle scars he bears are suddenly glaringly obvious. My failed relationships left me scarred, as well, including the unhealed wound of feeling like work was the real love of my husband's life.

"I'll tell you when I'm feeling neglected," I promise him. "And you'll drop everything for me then."

He lets that set in, visibly relaxing. Finally, he nods. "I'll fly out early Wednesday, then take a red-eye back Thursday night."

"Overnight flights are hell. Just plan on getting back here in the evening instead. I'll pick you up at the airport, and we can have dinner out."

"Then I'm looking at three days without you." He rubs his thumb over my lower lip. "And this amazing mouth."

"Do you ever not think about sex?"

Garrett grins. "Excuse me, but I was busy working when you marched up here and ripped my clothes off."

I wave that away. "You'll be gone two nights."

"Fine. But next time, you're coming with me."

"Next time, give me more notice."

"Deal."

I push to my feet. "Now put some clothes on."

"Think of all we can do with them off." He waggles his brows at me.

"You need help, Frost."

I listen with half an ear to him getting dressed while I stand and brush off my pants. Then I stop.

For the first time, I look at his work in progress. I go still.

His new canvas, resting on an easel, is considerably smaller than the previous one, which suits its more intimate tone. It is a searing, frenetic blend of crimson, orange, and yellow, with the faintest accents of aqua, green, and white. I am immediately reminded of a supernova—a brilliant burst of energy and power—and yet the shape is far earthier. And unquestionably more erotic.

I think of the painting hanging in his bedroom. That, too, is sensual. Sexy. But it lacks the immediacy of this new piece, as well as its colorfulness.

Garrett hugs me from behind. "I have no idea how I'm going to add what happened today to this. I may just have to give it a canvas of its own. Grab a paintball gun and just blast away. Boom. Like you did to my mind."

Part of me finds him silly and funny, while another part is awakening to the understanding that he's journaling our relationship through paint. He's revealing our sexual dynamic, which appears in his art as uniquely powerful, both destructive and renewing.

When Garrett's not working, he's with me. Apparently, when he is working, I'm also still with him, featuring heavily in his thoughts.

"You're not selling this." It's not a question.

"No." He bends and rests his chin on my shoulder. "We're hanging this one over our bed, in our bedroom, when that time comes."

I take a deep breath. Let it out. "What will you do with the other one?"

14

"Is it crazy that I'm this excited?" Roxy stage-whispers as we follow the event coordinator down a long hall in the Cross Tower Hotel.

"Maybe just a little. Eva's human, you know. Just like you and me. She brushes her teeth, has bad hair days, her skin breaks out."

"Girl, you're tripping," she scoffs. "Do I look okay?"

"Beyond okay. That outfit is perfection."

She's wearing a coral jumpsuit and white blazer. As usual, she looks chic and polished. A departure for her is the minimal accessories—diamond stud earrings and her wedding ring set.

We're shown into a ballroom with walls of windows on three sides, affording a panoramic view of Elliott Bay. The Seattle Great Wheel is to our left. A passing ferry moves out of view on the right. The room itself is decorated in various hues of gold, taupe, and sand, creating a luxurious space that complements the view rather than competes with it.

Cream table linens cover a sea of round tables. A crew is setting up lighting and cameras for a photo shoot with the view as a backdrop, along with a second setup in front of a neutral-color backdrop. There's a rack of clothes in the far corner, along with three director's chairs by a long table covered in cosmetics and hair-styling tools.

At another table nearby, a petite blonde in a white sleeveless sheath dress stands in bare feet next to a brunette wearing an elegant navy pantsuit, their heads bent over a pile of blown-up images.

Roxy grabs my hand and squeezes hard. "Oh my God, there she is. And look at that Chanel dress!"

Lifting her head, the blonde turns toward us, revealing a classically beautiful face. With her ever-changing hair now the palest shade of blond and styled in a sleek chignon, she reminds me of a glamorous leading lady from the Golden Age of Hollywood—Lana Turner or Tippi Hedren, maybe, with the overt sex appeal of Marilyn Monroe. She has the same curves.

"Teagan." Her smile makes her instantly approachable. "I'm so glad to see you."

Eva pads toward me, her hands held out to grip mine. Behind her, under the table, I spot a pair of sapphire stilettos. Large sparkling stones that I suspect are pink diamonds dangle from her ears, and another impressive diamond glitters from the ring finger of her left hand. She's got a Rolex on one wrist and a Chanel cuff on the other.

"How are you always more beautiful every time I see you?" she asks me, her husky voice filled with warmth. "I want to look that amazing without makeup. And this must be Roxy."

Roxy grabs Eva's hands. "I'm so happy to meet you!"

"The feeling's mutual." Eva's gray eyes are as soft as a foggy morning yet sharp with intelligence.

"And I love your new skin care line," Roxy goes on. "It's like a miracle. My skin hasn't been this plump and dewy in years."

"I forgot Teagan requested a set for you! I'm thrilled you like it. You've been using it for how long now?"

"A little shy of a month."

"If you're open to it, we could take some photos of you, too. We'd have to remove your gorgeous makeup, though, and I totally understand—"

"I'd love to!" Roxy gives an excited wiggle.

Eva laughs, and it's a rich, throaty sound that turns several heads in the room. "Great. This will be fun. After we're finished, the glam squad can make you back up again." Her gaze turns to me. "You look great just the way you are, Teagan, but you're welcome to use the glam squad, too, if you want. Up to you."

"I'll take all the help I can get."

"All right." She laughs again, then gestures at the photos on the table. "Come check out what we've done so far."

Roxy and I follow her, with Roxy pantomiming her excitement behind Eva's back. It's a struggle not to laugh.

Eva introduces us to Odeya, the brunette in navy, who turns out to be the advertising and marketing director of ECRA+. Then she waves her hand over the large photos mounted on sturdy foam core boards. We flip through a multitude of shots of women and men of various ages and ethnicities. All are styled with slicked-back hair and bare shoulders against a pale blush background. Some of the models are showcased with side-by-side before and afters.

Odeya flips to the next board. Roxy and I both hum our appreciation.

Gazing back at us from the photo is Eva's husband, Gideon, and her sister-in-law, Ireland. The siblings share the same striking traits: glossy black hair, thickly lashed blue eyes, and a perfection of features often used as wish lists by my former patients. Gideon's hair is cut to a rakish length that brushes the top of his powerful shoulders; Ireland's is a long fall of silk. They're posed with Ireland standing behind her older brother and slightly off to the side so that the full length of her tresses follows the curve of his biceps.

"Wow," Roxy says, leaning closer. "Look at the genetics at work there."

"I know," Eva says with a sigh. "And none of the photos has been retouched. No color correcting, no smoothing. That's just the way those two look all the time, although I like to think the ECRA+ system has added a little something to their natural glow."

Roxy glances at her. "Lucky you, girl. Your man is *fine*."

Eva's lovely mouth curves. "Isn't he? Seven years together, and I still pinch myself every morning."

"Don't rub it in," Odeya says, flipping to the next photo.

I smile when I recognize the very handsome man in the picture. "There's Cary."

Clapping softly, Roxy dips her knees in a little hop. "I love him! His posts on social media are hilarious."

"Tell me about it. There is no filter on that man," Eva says wryly. "He's the reason we're launching a men's care line in tandem with the main line. Cary reminded me that looking good is a universal desire."

Eva's best friend is more famous for being a social media phenomenon than a successful model, which doesn't mean he isn't drop-dead gorgeous. Married to a veterinarian and a frequent poster of ridiculously cute animal photos, he's best known for his insightful social commentary and biting comebacks. His followers, like Eva's, number in the tens of millions.

The next photo is also of Cary but includes a spectacular blonde. The two pair well together, his dark hair and green eyes a stunning contrast to her golden beauty. Both have enviable bone structure. They've been posed similarly to Gideon and Ireland, only this time, Cary stands behind the model.

"I know her," Roxy says, snapping her fingers as she racks her brain. "Tatiana Cherlin."

Eva nods. "That's right."

Roxy catches my eye. "She's the blonde I saw at Garrett's house just after he moved in. I thought she looked familiar, but I didn't place her until just now."

Startled by that, I look from Roxy's face back to the photo of Tatiana's unique, exotically beautiful face.

I'd totally forgotten Roxy mentioning a woman with Garrett. I had mentally deleted the information as some of Roxy's usual gossip, since I hadn't known it was Garrett who'd moved in next door at the time.

"They were together once," Roxy goes on, pointing at the photo. "Cary and Tatiana. They had a baby together, but he didn't survive. I remember it got a lot of press when it happened. That was a while back, though. Like, years ago."

I look at her, amazed at her storage capacity for tidbits from other people's lives and grateful that my level of notoriety isn't newsworthy enough to attract tabloid interest.

"It was shortly after I got married," Eva fills in quietly. "They're still struggling with it. Cary looks after her and probably always will. He asked me to consider including her in the campaign, and after trying ECRA+ for herself, she was happy to participate. Plus, she's always enjoyed working with Cary. Everyone does."

Odeya flips to the next image, a photo of Tatiana alone, and stops there for a few seconds. All three women are talking about the outrageous things Cary has posted in the past.

I have deliberately avoided thinking about what Garrett's life was like before he appeared next door. I've dodged thinking about a lot of things.

I stand beside Roxy, half listening. My thoughts are with the man presently preparing for an exhibition of his work on the other side of the country.

Among the crowd of travelers waiting at the curb outside of SeaTac's baggage claim, Garrett Frost is impossible to miss. He stands casually, one hand resting on the handle of his carry-on, the other holding his phone as he reads the screen. He's wearing black boots, black jeans, and a charcoal T-shirt, with a pair of black aviators on his handsome face.

It's not what he's wearing or even his unmistakable attractiveness that draws the eye first. It's his body: how confident his posture is, how easily he carries himself.

Chewing the inside of my lip, I carefully maneuver the Range Rover between idling vehicles to get as close as I can. His head lifts as I get ready to hop out. I can't see his eyes through his shades, but the pleasure he feels when he sees me is very clear. His face immediately breaks out into an intimate, sexy smile. I feel a little shiver of delight.

"Hey, you," I call out, hitting the button that opens the rear hatch before shutting the driver's side door. "How'd it go?"

He prowls toward me with that long-legged, purposeful stride that just does something to me. Instantly, heat flares through my body.

"As good as it possibly could go without you being there." Garrett does that fluid, effortless move to pull me into a kiss at the exact moment I realize that's his intent. His firm lips seal over mine, his tongue dipping in to stroke. A soft rumble of pleasure vibrates from his chest to mine. "I missed you," he tells me gruffly.

"I missed you more."

He gives me a triumphant smile. "Good. You want to drive?"

"No. This thing scares me. Why does a big SUV like this drive like a race car?"

He slides his suitcase into the cargo area and hits the button that automatically closes the hatch. "Five hundred and ten horses, powered by a supercharged V-8."

"That's crazy," I mutter, following him to the passenger side where he opens my door.

Garrett gives me a gentle swat on the butt as I climb in. "I'm liking those jeans on you, Doc. I'm liking them a lot."

I smile as he rounds the hood, pleased he noticed. I'd signed up for a styling subscription service after we started having sex, and my first box arrived while he was gone. Now I have at least a couple of outfits suitable for going out. It's progress, and I'm celebrating it.

He taps one of the memory buttons on the driver's side door and waits as the seat lowers and moves back from the wheel, making room for him to slide in. He adjusts the rear-view mirror and glances at me. "Where to?"

"You hungry?"

"Yep." He rakes me with a glance. "I could eat, too."

Shaking my head, I laugh, something that gets easier every day. "That was terrible."

"You liked it anyway." Looking over his shoulder, Garrett pulls out and away from the chaotic scrum of vehicles trying to pick up passengers. We leave the airport behind. "Where to?"

"How does Mexican sound?"

"I'm always down for good Mexican food."

"There's a place near here in Tukwila that has great reviews, or there's the one back in Federal Way, closer to home. I've been there; it's good."

"So let's go to Tukwila and try something new."

"Okay. Stay on 518 East."

He changes lanes, then reaches over the center console for my hand. "How'd work go?"

"Good. Roxy had a blast. Eva flew back to New York on a private jet that afternoon. I seriously thought about going with her and surprising you."

"Why didn't you?"

"Because we weren't going to get in until eleven, and I didn't know if you'd be at an after-party then or maybe out for a late dinner with friends." I shrug. "I didn't want to screw up whatever plans you might have arranged."

"I wouldn't have minded, Teagan. Not at all."

A speeding driver passes us, then cuts across recklessly to hop on the 5 South.

"I saw some of the photos that were posted." I look down at our joined hands. "I saw Tatiana Cherlin was there."

"She was, yes. She's a friend."

"Roxy told me Tatiana was with you when you moved in."

There's a moment of silence, then, "I feel like I'm getting ambushed here." He takes a deep breath. "She's a friend, that's it. She's never been more than that, and she's never going to be more than that for the very obvious reason that I'm in love with you and that's not going to change in this lifetime."

"Garrett . . ." Words are lost to me at that moment. I am a quivering mass of surprise, delight, and fear. My grip on his hand tightens.

"I met her at a support group for bereaved parents," he explains. "I was still in the weeds, and she'd already been wading through it for years. Talking to her made me realize it would get easier with time, that eventually I would learn to live with that level of agony."

"I'm glad she was there for you." I mean that sincerely. I think he can tell, because I see the tension in his body ease. "I wish I could have been."

He lifts my hand to his lips. "We're here for each other now. That's what counts."

"Does it bother you that you haven't been able to talk about David with me?"

Garrett waits a beat, then, "Let me turn that question around before I answer. Does it bother you when I talk about David?"

"No. It's just . . . *I'm* not a talker. I'm a good listener, but I feel like it would be a problem if you were sharing personal things and I wasn't. I'm worried it's a wedge," I confess. "A need you have that I'm not filling."

His thumb glides back and forth over my skin. "I dropped in for therapy while I was in the city. A lot has happened over the past few months: moving, getting back to making art, starting over with you. I felt like I should touch base."

I gesture toward our exit, and he changes lanes.

"There are things about my old life I miss, beyond just David," he says quietly. "But there are things happening now, between us, that make me happier than I've ever been. I feel guilty about that sometimes."

The maroon minivan in front of us has a BABY ON BOARD plaque in the rear window. It sways from side to side as it dangles from a suction cup.

"Dr. Petersen suggested we try journaling the things we can't—or don't want to—say," Garrett goes on, "and that we leave the journals open to be read. Takes talking out of the equation but still keeps the lines of communication open."

He glances at me when we stop at a light. "I picked up a couple of journals at the airport on the way back."

My eyes burn a little as I nod again. "Okay. Let's try."

"I know you don't like talking things out, but Dr. Petersen does video chats, too, if you decide differently."

I imagine talking about how I feel, and my stomach knots. Still, I nod. "I have a doctor, but I'll keep that recommendation in mind."

We turn toward the mall. The parking lot is crammed with vehicles. People and families hustle in and out of the myriad restaurants and stores. I used to feel so alone at times like these, confronted with how life marches on while I feel frozen in place.

I look at the man sitting beside me, holding my hand, working so hard to make us work out, and I appreciate how I don't feel the slightest bit lonely anymore. The ever-present sadness that isolated me from the world is a connecting tie with Garrett.

I place my other hand atop our handclasp. "By the way . . . I'm in love with you, too."

15

"I haven't been here in ages," Roxy says as we walk into Chihuly Garden and Glass.

"I don't think it changes," Mike says, glancing at the gift shop adjacent to the entrance. "I think the displays are permanent."

"You guys didn't have to buy tickets to see it again," I protest, although it's already too late, since we paid our entrance fees through a kiosk outside. "We could've met up later."

"We want to see it again," Roxy assures me. "I really only remember the boats."

"I just remember that sea-life room," Mike says. "The octopi are pretty impressive."

"It's octopodes," Roxy corrects.

"What?" He shakes his head. "No, it's not."

"It is. Look it up."

Mike pulls out his phone. A moment later, "I'll be damned. You're right."

"Of course I am."

Garrett throws an arm around my shoulders as we wait to show our tickets to a staff member. It's a gorgeous summer day, a bit on the warm side for Seattle, but thankfully nothing like the soupy humidity of New York at this time of year.

I'm wearing one of the outfits from my latest style box, a pair of white denim shorts and a strappy tank top with a pretty Asian-inspired pattern. I even put on earrings, a pair of small gold hoops, and went with a smoky eye, which has become my new normal. To my mind, a rock-star artist like Garrett pairs well with sultry eyes.

Making our way inside the museum, we weave through the crowds as we admire each exhibit. We reach a long, narrow room where the display is suspended above us, held up and protected by a clear barrier. Multicolored glass sculptures of various shapes and sizes, some floral in design, others aquatic, are scattered about, entwined or piled atop one another. Light filters through from above, casting rainbow shards of light against the bare walls.

Head tilted back, I move slowly so I can take in everything.

Garrett's hands catch me around the waist from behind, and he whispers, "We should go see his installation at the Bellagio in Las Vegas. Maybe kick off a honeymoon there before traveling to parts unknown."

I pause midstep, unsure if I heard him right. I turn to face him. "Did you just propose?"

His gorgeous eyes twinkle at me. "No. You won't be confused when I do. Just putting it out there. Giving you some time to warm up to the idea."

My gaze narrows. "Maybe I'll get around to asking the question first."

He grins. "A race it is, then."

"You two are spending more time looking at each other than you are at the art," Mike teases, passing by us with Roxy on his arm.

"Can't help being drawn to the most beautiful thing in the room." Garrett catches me by the elbow and leads me through to the next exhibit.

I lean into him. "How is it that you get hotter *and* cornier by the day?"

He winks at me. "Dedication, Doc. And natural talent."

As the morning moves on, we visit the Space Needle, taking photos on the clear plexiglass benches on the revamped observation deck, and MoPOP, where we spend most of our time in the Prince exhibition. Then we wander through the outdoor spaces of Seattle Center, where we stumble upon the Polish Festival in progress at the Armory and Mural Amphitheatre.

Onstage, couples in colorful folkloric costumes dance to lively music. Food booths surround the lawn where attendees sit on picnic blankets and folding chairs, while a special area has been sectioned off to create a beer garden. I spot crafting tables for kids, vendors of T-shirts and gifts, art displays, and more.

"Let's grab a drink," Roxy says, looking at the beer garden.

We make our way over to the white picket fence that defines the space, finding an empty table shaded by an umbrella advertising a Polish brew. Roxy and I take a seat.

"I'm grabbing a beer," Mike tells Roxy. "You want one? Or wine?"

"Wine sounds good."

Garrett looks at me. "Want a water or soda?"

"Um . . ." I smile. "I think I'll have a glass of wine, too. A chardonnay if they have it."

Roxy claps. "Watch out, Garrett. She's getting wild now."

He smiles. "It's okay, I can handle her."

As the men walk away, Roxy grabs my arm and leans forward. "Okay, Mike's been telling me to leave it alone, but I have to ask: Were you guys talking marriage back at the Chihuly museum?"

I shoot her a look. "In an abstract way. Don't get excited."

"Oh my God." Her eyes tear up. "I'm so happy for you. So happy for you both."

"Roxy, what did I just say? We're not engaged. We're still doing the same thing we were."

"But it's like a foregone conclusion. And that makes me so happy. When I think about what that man has been through, that he would find someone like you . . . And I think about the guys I tried to set you up with." She covers her face and gives a watery laugh. "You were so right to wait for Garrett to come along."

"Roxy, come on." I can't help but laugh, too. "Mike's going to freak out if he sees you crying."

"I know." She digs into her cross-body bag and pulls out a packet of tissues. "I'm a hopeless romantic—what can I say?"

"What's going on?" Mike says, coming back to the table with wine in one hand and a beer in the other. He looks at his wife and the tissues she's holding. "What's the matter?"

"Allergies, that's all. I'm cracking jokes about Teagan getting drunk."

I pull out the seat next to me for Garrett, and he sinks lithely into it, setting down our drinks in front of us. His hand goes to my thigh, warming my bare skin.

"Save me," I tell him.

He grins. "I'm working on it."

I had only the one glass of wine, but a year of abstinence has turned me into a lightweight. I feel a bit giddy, and laughter comes readily. Roxy, Mike, and Garrett all had two drinks, but I'm pretty sure they're much more sober than I am.

Garrett has an indulgent smile on his face as we continue wending our way through Seattle Center, his hand in mine. We stop and buy ice cream from a cart, then continue on, turning a corner to find ourselves facing the International Fountain. As we approach, music and children's laughter compete with the sound of splashing water.

Set within an expansive lawn, the fountain itself is a silver dome centered in a giant bowl. Visitors sit around the lip and lower, too, on the angled sides. Children and adults alike frolic amid the streams of water, some fully dressed, others in swimsuits.

"I love this place," Roxy says, her eyes shielded behind cat-eyed sunglasses. "It always feels like it's filled with joy."

She leads us to the edge and takes a seat, her legs stretched down toward the fountain. Mike joins her.

Tense, I look at Garrett. "You okay?"

He nods, the playing children reflected in his mirrored shades. "I'm good."

Offering his hand for balance, he waits for me to take a seat before joining me. We sit side by side, eating our ice cream. The instrumental music playing is unfamiliar to me, which makes it possible for me to listen to it. Garrett listens to music a lot when he's working, and I'm slowly getting used to it again. There are still moments when a song reminds me of a place or event that hurts me to recall, but I'm making progress there, too.

Day by day, I'm peeling back layers and tackling new challenges.

"David!"

My whole body stiffens at the sound of a woman calling that name. I look at Garrett, making sure he's all right. He reaches over and grips my hand, giving it a reassuring squeeze.

My gaze returns to the fountain, searching. I see a redhead brandishing a towel, chasing a ginger-haired boy about five years of age who has no interest in leaving. Licking my mint chocolate chip ice cream, I follow the little drama as it plays out.

Despite the crowd, I'm not doing too badly when another boy appears from where he was hidden on the other side of the fountain. This one is older, maybe seven or eight. Dark-haired, dark-eyed, square-jawed. He laughs while chasing a little girl in a pink leotard with attached tutu. They're both soaked and barefoot.

Melting ice cream runs down my fingers as I stare. The little boy is tall for his age and thin. His lashes are thick and spiked with water, his tongue darting out to lick around his mouth. Aside from the eyes, he looks so much like Garrett that my brain can hardly process it.

Heart pounding, I push to my feet.

"Doc?"

Garrett's voice sounds far away, making it easy to ignore. I start down the slanted side of the bowl.

Roxy laughs behind me. "I think she's going in!"

Mike says something in answer.

"Teagan." Garrett's voice has an edge now.

"Do you see him?" I ask as I move away. "Do you see him?"

"Teagan!"

I reach the bottom. The wind blows a spray of water at me, wetting me from head to toe. Children run all around me, darting forward and back as they play tag with the shooting water. The little ballerina runs by, and the dark-haired boy is hot on her heels.

"Excuse me," I call out, but he runs off, having no clue I'm talking to him.

Garrett grabs my arm, pulling me back when I start forward. "What the hell are you doing?"

"Do you see him? He looks like David."

His jaw tightens. "Let's get out of here."

"Not yet."

He grabs my upper arms and gives me a little shake. My ice cream falls to splatter in the water at my feet. "That's not David."

"I know that. You haven't even looked at him." Turning my head, I see the boy again and point. "See? He looks just like you, with my eyes. He's the right age."

Roxy joins us. "Is everything all right?"

"We have to go," Garrett says tightly. "Teagan's tired."

"I'm not tired," I argue. "I just want to talk to him for a minute."

"You can't talk to that boy!" he snaps. "You're a stranger to him. You'll freak him out. You'll freak his parents out. We have to go."

"Garrett, you don't—"

Shoving his sunglasses on top of his head, his tearful gaze meets mine. "He's not our son, Teagan. He's not our David. David's dead."

Those two words pierce through my chest. Garrett's ravaged expression is painful to look at. His face blurs as hot tears spill down my cheeks.

"I know he's dead!" I yell at him, sobbing, as another chilling mist of water douses us both. "You don't have to *tell* me that."

I've held back tears for so long. Now that they're freed, I can't stop them. "I know that's not him. I know . . . God, am I crazy?"

"Come here." Garrett pulls me into his arms, holding me unbearably close.

As my tears soak into his T-shirt, his body shakes against mine.

16

GARRETT

I stand on the threshold of one of three bedrooms on the daylight basement level of Teagan's home. Just the sight of the room is so painful, I can't enter it.

Here is David's bed, perfectly made. Here is his bookshelf and toy box. His clothes hang in the closet. Framed photos I recognize from our former life are scattered around the room: our wedding photo, a photo taken moments after David's birth, birthday pictures, school pictures, vacation photos.

Why have I never come down here before now?

Shutting the door, I look at the second living room on this lower floor. Like the upstairs, it's perfectly retro and completely sterile. Only the one bedroom holds any of the woman I love in it.

The sound of a soft, tentative knock on the front door drifts down the stairs. I take the steps two at a time up to the main floor, wanting to answer it before the doorbell can ring and wake Teagan. Pulling the door open, I'm not at all surprised to see Roxanne.

"Hi," she greets me quietly. "How are you doing? Is Teagan okay?"

All the light I'm used to seeing in Roxy is gone. I sigh. We'll have to repair this relationship, too. Grief is like a shattered mirror, the central break spreading cracks throughout.

"She's sleeping." I wave my hand toward the kitchen. "I'm about to have a drink. Want to join me?"

"Sure." She comes in and looks around, as if she expects the place to look different.

I head to the kitchen. "I grabbed scotch from my place, but she's got a bottle of wine in the fridge."

Roxy huffs a humorless laugh. "I gave her that bottle when she moved in. Think it's still good?"

"We can find out." The product of an Australian winery, the bottle has a screw-on cap. I open it, sniff, then pour some into a glass and take a sip. "Yeah, it's fine."

She accepts the glass I pour her, taking a decent swallow while I pour a hefty slug of scotch for myself. I join her at the table.

Her gaze settles on me. "I'm really confused."

"I bet." I take a long drink, feeling the alcohol go down in a burst of heat.

"Is Teagan your wife?"

"She was. We divorced a few months after we lost David."

"Oh." She wraps her hands around her wineglass. "I suppose that happens a lot after the death of a child."

"That's a myth." I hear the bite in my voice and regret it instantly. "I'm sorry."

"It's okay."

I continue, my tone softer, "Only sixteen percent of couples divorce, and usually it's not because of the loss; it's because things weren't right anyway, and the child was the glue holding the marriage together." I take another drink. "At least that's how it was for us."

Roxy also takes another drink, then plays with the stem of her glass. "She seemed surprised when you two first ran into each other."

"Yeah, well, I was even more surprised when you introduced her to me and she didn't correct you. Pissed me the fuck off, actually. It felt like she'd completely erased our entire life together, just wiped it out of existence." I take another drink, rolling the liquor around in my mouth before swallowing. "After I was done yelling at my therapist about it, he explained something called 'complicated grief.'"

"I just read about that the other day."

I nod. "Once I understood that she not only hadn't moved on but was still in the weeds with it, I knew she needed me as much as I needed her."

"I had no idea," she says quietly.

"I was afraid to tell you."

We both turn our heads at the sound of Teagan's voice. She stands on the threshold of the kitchen, looking pale and puffy-eyed. I'd helped her into an oversize T-shirt after getting her out of the ice cream–stained clothes she'd been wearing. She looks small and lost, the smattering of freckles across her cheeks and nose visible against her pale skin.

I stand and go to her, brushing the hair back from her face. She sobbed the whole way home, racking, violent cries that ripped my heart out.

"I'm okay," she tells me, her hands circling my wrists. Her makeup has smeared, surrounding her eyes with dark smudges.

She's so beautiful. I've been sketching her face for years in notebooks, on napkins, on junk mail. I could draw the oval of her face, the rise of her cheekbones, and the almond shape of her eyes while blindfolded.

"I'm sorry about what happened at the fountain, Garrett."

My lips brush her forehead. "Don't apologize."

"I don't know what got into me." She gives an awkward shrug. "I want to sit down."

I pull a chair out for her, then go to the kitchen to get her a glass of juice.

Roxy bites her lower lip, clearly not knowing what to say or do.

"I needed you to be my friend, Roxy," Teagan explains quietly. "So many of our friends disappeared after we lost David, and the ones who stuck around never looked at us the same. It gets to be too much. The pitying looks. People treating you like you're going to snap at any minute. The way no one laughs. It's hard to carry that extra load when you're already feeling crushed."

Roxy is crying when I come back to the table and set the glass of orange juice in front of Teagan.

"I can't be mad at you," Roxy says, wiping her face with her hands. "Not after the way I freaked out when Garrett talked about David. It just makes me so sad thinking of you living with that all on your own. And I'm sure I must've said hurtful things without even realizing it."

I rip a paper towel off the roll and take it to her.

She looks up at me. "Thank you. You two really are back together, though, right? That's for real?"

My attention turns to Teagan. She's been opening like a flower over the past few weeks, but now she's once again subdued. Still, there's a new steadiness in her gaze. I find myself holding out hope that she's turned a corner. And if she hasn't, well . . . We'll get there. I know that for a certainty, and that's enough.

"It's all been real, Roxy," she replies earnestly. "There are some things you didn't know, but everything you do know is absolutely the truth."

Teagan's gaze finds mine for an instant of connection before she looks back at her friend. "We've changed enough to make it work this time, I think. I didn't expect it. When Garrett wrote to me, asking if I was willing to try starting from scratch, I said yes only because I felt I owed David that much. We were so broken when we divorced . . . we'd fallen out of love somewhere along the way."

"I still loved you," I counter, standing by the island because I can't sit down. It's hard enough just trying to stand still. "I agreed to the divorce because I wanted you to be happier. You'd already gone through hell with Kyler when we met. I didn't want you feeling like you'd escaped one bad marriage only to get stuck in another."

She frowns. "When you didn't put up a fight, I figured you were done."

Roxy glances from Teagan to me and back again. She looks embarrassed but fascinated, and I don't care that she's witnessing this overdue discussion. Because she's here, sticking by Teagan, giving support.

"We'd been fighting enough." I ran a hand over my jaw, remembering those dark, painful days. "After I got my head on straight, I realized that if you weren't happy, the answer wasn't letting you go. The answer was to try harder."

Teagan stares at me for a long minute.

"I'm going to go." Roxy stands. "Mike and I would really love it if you both came over for dinner tomorrow. He told me to tell you it's been too long since he made pizza."

A tear slides down Teagan's cheek. "We wouldn't miss Mike's pizza."

"Great." Roxy heads to the sink, but I intercept the glass from her.

"I'll take care of it."

She cups my face in her hands and presses a kiss to my cheek. "Call me if you need anything."

Teagan and I watch her leave; then I go to the sink and wash the glass, setting it in the drain basket. I jump when Teagan's arms circle me from behind, then relax into the embrace. Her cheek presses against my back. I wrap my arms over hers.

"What's next?" she asks, her breath soft and warm as it drifts across my skin.

"Hmm . . . Dinner?"

She pulls back, and I turn to face her. I can see so much of our son in her features, her mannerisms, her laugh. I've realized over the past weeks that he's still with us, in little and big ways.

"I'll cook," she offers.

I feel the last of my tension drain away. "Yeah?"

"I'll make spaghetti. You always liked my spaghetti."

"I do. I'm looking forward to having it again." Such an understatement. To be able to revisit our past, even something as simple as a favorite meal she used to make for our family, is something I've longed for until it was a hollow ache inside me.

Her hands run lightly up and down my arms, her gaze on the art that covers them. "This must have hurt."

"That was the point at first."

Teagan looks up at me. "I think your tattoos are very sexy."

"I'm glad to hear that." Heat rivaling the burn of the scotch spreads through me.

"Is there a meaning to the design?"

I nod. "They're mazes. One begins and ends at my heart; the other begins and ends at the pulse point on my right wrist."

Her eyes widen as she takes that in, her gaze following the swirls and angles of the designs.

"David was my lifeblood," I explain. "You're my heart. Whatever twists and turns life takes, everything begins and ends with you both."

Tears glisten in her eyes but don't fall. "I'm going to trace them both," she tells me, her voice husky with emotion. She grips my biceps for balance as she lifts to her toes to kiss my jaw.

"That might take a while," I point out. "Years, possibly."

"I'm not going anywhere." She rests her cheek on my chest.

"I love you," I tell her, my hands on her hips. Again, the words are an understatement, incapable of conveying the depth of emotion I feel.

Pulling back, Teagan smiles, and I see the brightness of it chase some of the shadows from her eyes.

"I love you more," she answers.

"I am totally okay with that." I lean back against the sink and pull her into the space between my spread legs, holding her close. I'll be holding her close until I take my last breath.

"One step at a time, right?" she murmurs.

"Yeah, Doc. That's how we'll do this. One step at a time."

ACKNOWLEDGMENTS

My thanks to Hilary Sares, for editing my rough draft.

Thanks to my agent, Kimberly Whalen, for wielding the sword while I wield my pen.

Thanks to my dear friend and fellow author Karin Tabke, for too many things to list here.

And thanks to my editor, Anh Schluep, for approaching me to write for her. The end result is this story. Teagan and Garrett mean so much to me. I'm grateful for the time I spent with them.

ABOUT THE AUTHOR

Photo © Meghan Poort

Sylvia Day is the #1 *New York Times*, #1 *USA Today*, #1 *Sunday Times*, #1 *Der Spiegel*, and #1 international bestselling author of over twenty award-winning novels sold in more than forty countries. She is a #1 bestselling author in twenty-eight countries, with tens of millions of copies of her books in print. Visit the author at www.sylviaday.com.